FLOATERS

Also by Kelli Owen

FLOATERS

Kelli Owen

Gypsy Press

Dedication: To Mary Shelley… She knows why. We've discussed it at length in many a library and late night.

Acknowledgements: Thanks (as always) to my empty nestlings Mark & Amanda (and her progeny: Raynebow, Thunder & Lightning); my hippie, Bob Ford, and his squatters Sauce & Nugget; Mom for research field trips and photos; Nana for blood & history lessons as a child; my prereaders of doom Tod, Kyle, & Syko Mike; Bryan, aka @TheRickGrimes_ on twitter for making me giggle and volunteering to die; and my readers, who always astound and amaze me with their love and affection—you humble me, and I humbly offer you this…

America is not a young land: it is old and dirty and evil.
Before the settlers, before the Indians...
The evil was there...
Waiting.
— William S. Burroughs

Beware; for I am fearless, and therefore powerful.
— Mary Shelley, *Frankenstein*

CHAPTER ONE

Carly Greene's phone buzzed a muted plea for attention from her pocket. She blinked, and lost the staring contest she'd been having with the remnants of lunch—three shot glasses coated in the ghosts of tequila and the last swig in an otherwise empty bottle of Miller Genuine Draft. She pulled her phone free and pushed the button to light up the notification screen. Curling her lip, Carly slumped in resignation and slid a twenty across the bar. She shoved the phone back in her pocket without responding to the message and nodded at the bartender.

"I'll be back, Jen. Lake Superior's coughing up her dead again."

The bartender grimaced, "I'll keep your seat warm, if you promise to keep the details to yourself."

Carly nodded and turned, squinting as she reached the beam of sunshine at the doorway. She almost ran into the silhouette of a man before she blinked the darkness of the bar away and sidestepped the approaching form in the doorway.

"Hey Carly…"

"Ah fuck, really, Parker? Not now." She shielded her eyes from the sun with her hand, and confirmed the face in front of her matched the voice. She knew it would. She'd know *that* voice underwater, in a coma, or otherwise.

"Did you hear about the bodies yet?"

Her annoyance washed away instantly. "Bodies? With an S?"

He nodded excitedly.

"You were listening to the scanner again, weren't you?"

"It's my job."

"No, your job is to report the news, not make shit

up based on a cheat sheet for scanner codes and your imagination."

"Ouch, Carly. That hurt."

"Not as much as…" She huffed and held back her venom. "I have shit to do. All I know, all I can tell you *on the record*, is I'm needed at the mouth of the Nemadji." She turned and headed for her unmarked black sedan.

"I'll follow you."

Carly pretended not to hear the Evening Telegraph reporter, sidestepping puddles on her way to the car.

She pulled out of the Keyport Lounge parking lot and turned east on Belknap Avenue. The text message hadn't said 911, so she drove without slapping the magnetic emergency light onto her roof. It would take ten minutes to get through downtown, onto Highway 2, and out to the Superior-Allouez border marked by the Nemadji River. Carly let her mind wander as far as she could from the reporter visible in her rearview mirror.

She noted the waterlogged lawns, brim-filled drainage ditches, and dark bottomless puddles as she drove. The spring had been fast and furious. Between the thick lake ice melting too fast as temperatures rose too quickly, to the heavy rains having nowhere to soak into because the ground was still frozen and hard as a rock. *Souptown* really was rather soupy at the moment. Carly thought, *and as usual, when the thaw happens too fast, that bitch of a "great" lake floats something up from the depths of winter's abyss.*

Carly remembered the summer her family had moved from Ashland to Superior's East End, and she found herself suddenly within walking distance of what was officially only the inner bay. The bay, the inlet, the outer current, the lighthouse stretch—it was all the same to her, no matter the particular area, no matter the technical name, it was all Lake Superior. And Carly had learned at a very early age the lake was no lady, and had a hell of a temper.

She'd been witness to incredible storms, which had raged stronger than they should merely because of the lake's ability to make weather worse if it hovered above her for too long. She'd been frightened into her parents' room in the middle of the night when she was younger and onto the couch as she grew. She'd heard of, but never been victim to, the *small craft warnings*, which really meant *get your ass off the lake*. And the year she turned eleven, at the end of summer, Carly learned what the lake was capable of coughing up. Memories. Pain. Death.

A little girl who had been missing for almost twenty years had washed onto the shore near Barker's Island—an artificial island no more than a stone's throw off the mainland. Barker's Island housed a marina, hotel, an ore boat turned museum, a ferry for tourists, several swimming and fishing holes used by the young and stubborn, and was only three blocks from Carly's new house. She'd simply followed the sirens that day, and joined the crowd of onlookers on the wet sand.

Rather than being pulled from the depths by the thawing ice of spring, little Sarah Jane Preston's body had been dragged from her resting place by a vicious late season storm. The storm had raged for hours the night before, and been responsible for uprooting trees and subsequently overturning sidewalks in those heavy roots. It churned the lake and sky alike, until it pulled the girl from the muck, which had been dredged to no avail twenty years beforehand.

Carly shuddered as she remembered the vision. The dress tattered by age and rot, but still whole enough to be described, the pattern of tiny blue flowers still vividly clear in Carly's mind. The girl's blond hair had been leeched to an almost translucent state during her time beneath the frigid waves—the deepest of the great lakes never actually achieved what tourists would call "warm." She remembered the cop tripping in the wet sand and jarring the body, causing the head to roll toward the onlookers, sending a squeal of horror through the crowd and giving Carly nightmares for months.

That was the day Carly learned Lake Superior was just as capable of giving as she was of taking. That was the first time Carly had heard the term "floater" in reference to the dead occasionally coughed up from the depths of the great lake.

Today, *she* was the cop. Hopefully she wouldn't trip in the sand and cause nightmares.

Carly noted the squad car on the side of the road directly across from the Nemadji Travel Plaza, which was just a Kwik Trip station with an ego. She parked with hazard lights on just shy of the bridge crossing the mouth of the Nemadji River. A young officer nodded at her, as she pulled in behind him and got out. She walked toward him without paying attention to the sound of the car door behind her, which she knew to be Parker.

"Detective," the officer addressed her and spun on a heel, "this way."

"Where's the old man?" Carly noticed the beat cop's partner was missing, as she pulled her black hair back and put the elastic band she kept on her wrist around it in a quick pony tail.

"I'm solo this week, Ben's got court. Two separate cases, one could go for days. So if you need any extra help with this, I'm all yours."

Even through his standard patrol uniform of crisp blue pants and a starched button-up shirt, she could tell the young officer's frame was thin, if not what would be considered *rail*. But she knew his family, and knew their build, and was fully aware hiding under fabric meant to portray authority were wiry muscles and probably a couple well placed but regrettable tattoos. The uniform somehow made his family's normally tough appearance seem softer, kinder, almost vulnerable—quite the opposite of what a cop needed to portray to the public. Then again, she'd seen him in action as well, and when emergency struck, he was exactly the cop you wanted nearby. Except today. Today he didn't look ready to protect and serve.

"You okay, Babybird? You look a bit pale." She hoped the nickname she'd given him the previous summer—after he stopped traffic to rescue a fallen nest, only to find it empty—would lighten his mood.

He looked over his shoulder and gave her half a smile, Carly wasn't sure if it was to reassure her he was fine or because the nickname made him smile at his own embarrassment.

"You know, I'm fine with criminals, thugs, crooks, even wayward teens with something to prove. I can handle the parts of the job I joined for, but I hate the bodies. It's just gross. I don't know. And for some reason, floaters are grosser to me than fresh death."

"I get that. The color, the long dead emptiness in the eyes—"

"No, it's the stink. They smell way different. The rot doesn't smell… human."

"Well, they *are* human. And they usually have families we have to notify, so keep that in mind."

The smell hit her and she paused a moment, long enough for Parker to run into the back of her.

"Sorry. I didn't mean to get that clo—"

"Just back up." She pulled away from his splayed hands on her back. "Look around, Parker. No one else is here. You can get the exclusive without being in the way."

Carefully leaning back as she headed down the slope of the bank to the river below, Carly could hear the water in the muddy grass squishing and prayed she wouldn't lose her footing. When she heard the slip, thud and murmured cussing behind her, she smiled at Parker's fate. Rather than turning to help him, she simply called out, "You okay back there?"

"Yeah. Christ. I'm fine."

His voice trailed off as Carly stopped next to the young officer, Mikey Gunderson, the present half of the squad partners of Babybird and Ben Sparkman, Sparky to those who knew him long enough to get away with it. Ben would have given Babybird serious shit if he'd been present to see his sour expression.

Then she sniffed and looked around the river's edge. "You weren't kidding about the smell, were you? Jesus that's ripe for…" She looked down at the carnage, "Well, even for *two* bodies."

She reached past the notebook in her pocket and chose her iPhone instead. Carly began to take pictures, careful to use her zoom rather than get too close and knock things out of place.

There were two bodies, or rather, as Carly noted with both a grimace and the first of several photos, a body and a half. Between the normal rot, the extensive corrosion waterlogging did to human flesh, and the time of year, the bodies were in terrible shape. They looked far more skeletal than any floaters Carly could think of and she wondered how long the lake had held them under before their sour taste caused her to spit them up into Carly's life.

Carly presumed the first of the two to be female.

The lower half was gone, torn or simply decayed at the hips, while the remnants of a thin white shirt covered the torso. While flattened with death, age, and rot, the fact there had once been breasts on its chest was evident by the visible bra strap still clinging to the skeletal rib cage, under a shirt which was likely see-through even when dry. Most of the flesh on the female victim's face had been chewed or pulled free by the river's inhabitants, leaving an almost clean skull with bits of long black hair clinging to it in random clumps.

Carly guessed the second victim as male by his frame, angular facial structure, and clothing. His flesh—or what little was left, stuck to soggy pieces of fabric and glued to joints by ligaments not eaten by fish—was a medium to dark brown, like a coffee-stain on white cloth, rather than the deep rich brown of jerky. His eyes were gone, as was the flesh around his mouth, making his face look more skeletal with large black holes for eye sockets and what seemed to be a macabre grin. She wasn't surprised and knew this particular kind of damage usually meant spring or fall, rather than winter.

She glanced at the broken bits of wood around the body, planks she would normally presume to be fragments of an ice shack, but something wasn't right. "This look like canoe wood to you? It's not an ice-fishing accident, the fish nibbles are all wrong for cold water and that's not shack boards."

"Well, we're on the west side of the bridge here. Doesn't the river flow out? Wouldn't that mean they came from the river rather than the lake? The river is shallow and gets colder right? Could still be a shack…"

"No, actually, the river has enough current that it doesn't properly freeze over most winters—a thin sheen at best with a still-flowing current underneath. Not thick enough to hold a structure let alone people inside it. Which means it's definitely not a shack unless it came from *way* upstream. So again, I have to question, canoe?" She shook her head as she spoke trying to place the wood.

"That wood?" Parker was pointing to the planks near the water's edge.

Carly nodded and Gunderson nudged one with his foot, before pulling his foot back and giving Carly an apologetic look for moving evidence.

"It's not curved. That's not boat wood. Hell, that could be a bridge plank. You know how the kids will put random planks across the narrow parts upstream? Could just be some of those. I mean, how do you know they're connected to the bodies?"

"You're right. We don't. Now please step back a bit, Parker." She turned to Mikey, "You call this in or just text me?"

"Both. Dispatch said get you down here and then have you call in with deets once you checked it out. Said something about you loving Floaters." He gave her a strange quizzical look as if he didn't believe what he'd been told.

Carly snarled, "Asshole. Lemme guess, Lucas was on?"

Mikey nodded, "And playing a joke on both of us, I gather."

"Yeah… not us, just me, but it's okay, I'll get him back."

She glanced between the bodies as she continued snapping pictures from different angles and heights, occasionally squatting for a different perspective.

"These are really chewed up, and not new. The boards would normally make me think it was a shack, but something isn't right. Can you check reports for missing persons and ice fishing accidents from further upriver, maybe up near Pattison where the ice gets thicker? Actually, *any* missing persons near the river, throughout the county, in case those boards are from a boat or handmade bridge." Carly shook her head at the dead, thinking. "I can't tell how old they are, maybe the morgue can do that. There's nothing left here at this point, for us or even forensics—never is when they wash up like this, any evidence is long gone—so call the baggers. They can tag 'em and get 'em to Donny and then we'll know more."

"You going to the autopsy?" Officer Gunderson's tone sounded curious but partly disgusted.

"Not while he's actually doing it, unless Donny calls me in. Otherwise I let him do his thing and just give me the report when he's done. No need for me to be near this crap once it heats up and the stink really kicks in." She wiped a hand at the invisible stench in front of her nose.

Mikey nodded at her insinuation, "Gotcha. All right, I'll call for bags and wait for them, meanwhile I'll go see what I can find in the car computer for missing persons and let you know."

"Thanks, I'm going back to lunch."

"That's what you're calling it?" Parker had listened to their exchange while scribbling in his notebook and looked up at Carly with a raised eyebrow when she announced her intentions.

The green in his hazel eyes was strong against the overcast sky and she felt a flutter of familiarity in her gut. Carly brushed past him, hoping the rough contact would cause him to lose his balance again. She reached her car and quickly slid inside, pulling the door shut and locking out the world. She saw Parker get in his car, do a U-turn off the edge of the road, and head back into town. She gripped the wheel until her knuckles went white and lowered her head to rest on them.

In the nose, out the mouth.

She practiced what she preached a handful of times before sitting back up, starting the engine, and heading back to the bar.

CHAPTER TWO

Carly was staring at her notebook, laying open in front of her. The shot glass next to it was as empty as the blank page. She subconsciously tapped the rim of it with her fingernail, as she waited to hear from the morgue or Officer Gunderson.

"So, tell me about him."

Carly looked up to see Parker sliding into the chair across from her at the little round table. She silently cursed *him* as much as she did the full barstools she'd found upon returning, as the seating choice had provided privacy she didn't want to share with him.

"Who?" She was amazed he couldn't just understand she wanted—no *needed*—to be left alone. His dirty blonde hair—a touch too shaggy to be professional but not long enough to be considered artsy—showed signs of dampness at the ends, and she figured he'd taken a quick shower to get the hillside mud off him.

"The boy who put you here. The boy who put that expression on your face." He raised his eyebrows slowly, his hazel eyes widening with fake innocence, and she realized he was trying to be playful. "The boy who broke your heart?"

"I don't think so, Parker. Not today." She was sure the look she shot him was making her eyes darken. Normally a light brown, often referred to as amber, they changed when she was truly angry or upset, and then they tended to deepen to a rich chocolate brown. She was both at the moment.

"Fine. Can I buy you a drink?"

Every part of her wanted to scream 'no' at the top of her lungs, cause a scene that would embarrass him, and shun him into leaving. Instead, she flicked her empty shot glass his direction, "Sure."

He put down the replacement shot he already had in his hand. For some reason, even though she'd seen it and knew he'd been dry as of late, she'd thought it was his. Maybe because anyone who'd just seen those bodies wouldn't be blamed for wanting a drink. Or maybe he'd gone back to the bottle. Didn't matter. She nodded a thank you, slammed the shot, and put the empty glass inside the first empty.

"So, how's life at the paper?" She purposely set the direction of conversation toward him.

"Same old, same old. They try to assign me boring stories, and I try to turn in other things. As long as I'm getting paid for the boring and they're on Saul's desk with time to spare, he doesn't care. I think some days he appreciates it more than he let's on. I mean, really, how can he find neighborhood garage sales and local school events exciting?"

"They hate printing negative things about the lake— bad for tourism and all that, according to his all-mighty cousin, the mayor. No way is he going to let you cover the floaters we just saw."

"Sure he will, he just won't realize it's about floaters. I'll make it a human interest piece about safety near the water and slip the corpses past as a dangerous example of the consequences."

He smirked, and she winced, expecting his little obnoxious chuckle when he was proud of himself for something. She was spared. He excused himself instead.

Carly watched him walk to the bar as if he were the only person in the room, stand at the end and patiently wait for Jen to notice him. A nod between reporter and bartender was all that was needed, and Jen pushed over a shot glass of clear liquid, a freshly opened MGD, and a glass of ice water with a lemon wedge on the edge of the glass. Deftly picking up the neck of the beer bottle and shot glass with one hand, he grabbed the water with the other and returned. Putting the alcohol in front of her, he returned to his seat. She raised her eyebrow at the shot glass.

"If you're going to drink poison, at least show some class and drink silver instead of Jose's piss." He nodded to the shot glass of clear liquid.

"There's the know-it-all snark I've been missing."

"Not snarky. Just… you have less headaches with the silver."

"Ass." Carly picked up the shot glass, and paused. She almost looked like she was enjoying the aroma, like it was a fine wine aged in some fancy French basement, rather than the mass-produced 1800 Silver pretending to be the champagne of tequila.

"I know." His eyes went between hers and the shot glass hovering by her mouth.

"Just like that boy." She put the glass down and grabbed the beer instead, taking a swig without taking her eyes off Parker.

He dropped his gaze to the table for a moment then looked back up at her, meeting her eyes with a soft expression she wasn't sure how to label.

"You know, I trusted that boy. The *fucking* boy who did this to me? I trusted him." She put her arms on the table in front of her, palms down, fingers splayed, and leaned toward him. "Here he was, my best friend for *years*. I mean, my *best* friend. No matter what. Through everything. So when he said we should try more it seemed logical. He said the juice was worth the squeeze. And because I trusted him, I believed him."

She wondered if he could see the twitch beginning at

the corner of her eye.

"It was great. It was easy and fun and natural. It was that thing no girl really believes exists but we all secretly hope to find. There it was. In front of me. I had what every Disney princess promised… And I was *happy*. Truly, fucking, *at my core*, happy."

Carly sighed and took another drink of beer, this time it was a long healthy pull rather than a quick swig to chase a shot.

"Trust is a funny thing." She wiped the corner of her mouth as if she'd dribbled beer. "It's intangible. It's not real. You can't touch it, but you can sure break it. Some people hand it out like party favors—everyone gets some. Other people will make you work for it. Earn it. *Prove* you deserve it. Either way, when it's broken… When it's gone…" Her voice faded to a whisper, "I trusted him."

She looked down at the bottle of beer in her hand. "Of all the people in the whole world. I even trusted him more than my parents, and they're my *parents*—you're *supposed* to be able to trust them, you're *supposed* to be able to believe in them, and I do. But I trusted him *more* than that. I willingly gave that kind of faith and belief to a person, and he *promised* to hold it close. Promised to never *ever* be careless with my heart. And then to just… go and… well…"

Carly realized she was rambling into her beer and looked up at Parker. "I'm not so sure the juice was worth it. Seems I wasn't the only fruit on the tree."

Parker blinked, but kept eye contact. His hand was frozen on the water glass, as it dripped condensation down his fingers.

Carly lowered her eyes. "He broke my trust. He broke his promises. And in doing so, he broke a piece of me, a part of me deep inside. He broke my belief. My soul. And

22

I don't even know *how* to bandage it. Let alone if it'll ever heal." She looked up at him, narrowing her eyes in the dim light. "*That. That's* what he did."

Silence hung between them like a bubble, somehow kept separate from the ambient noises of the bar's other patrons, the television near the bar, and the hum of the air conditioning. Carly wondered if he could hear her heart, ticking off the seconds with an angry staccato. She watched him, hoping he wouldn't, but almost daring him to speak.

"I'm sorry, Carly. Can you forgive me? Can we try—"

"No." She stood and grabbed the tequila, gulped the shot, and slammed the empty down on the table in front of him. "I am *not* done being pissed."

She was out the door before he had a chance to say anything else, or see the tears threatening to break free. She held them back while she drove to the empty field that used to house the abandoned Catholic orphanage next to the dying strip mall. The overgrown surroundings hid vehicles well, as most teenagers and all cops knew, and she pulled into the late afternoon shadows.

Carly wasn't sure if she didn't know *how* to deal with the insane emotions battling inside her, or if she was just avoiding them. At the moment she wanted to simply shut down. She pulled out her cell phone to text Officer Gunderson for an update.

"Still going through the reports. Half the time the missing are found but the initial report isn't clearly marked to state that. I'll let ya know if I find something."

She answered with a simple "OK," and leaned back against the headrest.

In the nose, out the mouth.

She shut her eyes and lost track of time for a while.

• • • • •

Carly blinked several times. The kink in her neck and the darkness outside took a second for her to process, but when she did, she rolled her eyes at her own actions and reached forward to start the car. The radio came to life and let her know it was half past eight. Her phone had no notifications.

"Poor Babybird." She mused out loud at the number of records he must have found.

She pulled out from the behind the bushes, the only remaining foliage, in what used to be a grand turnaround driveway for a three-story orphanage run by the Catholic church. She paused, still blinking her stress nap away and wishing it had been more of a blackout-drunk nap. The moonlight lit the area around her like some B-horror movie and she smiled. The flat patch of out of place grass still looked strange to her, like an insult to the giant structure, which had stood for almost a century, but she found comfort on the property. The abandoned orphanage had been such a big part of her childhood growing up in East End. They had all trespassed on the land countless times and had each dared slip inside at least once. She remembered the haunted houses put on by the local JC's every year, and the eventful last time she'd gone, which had ended in tears of fear and her begging a costumed ghoul to get her out of there. Hell, she had even spent some illicit teenage hours in the shadow of the looming but forgotten building experimenting with boys and smoking—occasionally at the same time. And then they tore it down.

"Progress," she whispered to the dark interior of the car. "Progress kills memories." *And that damn lake coughs them back up,* she thought.

Carly drove the handful of blocks to the lake and stared at it from the red light she waited for. Rather than crossing to Barker's Island to continue her physical meandering, her mental wanderings turned her vehicle left and led her to the parking lot of the Holiday Inn, which Parker was currently calling home. She turned off the headlights and thought for a moment, wondering if she should apologize.

He hadn't just metaphorically asked for it, he had actually sat down and played cute and coy and acted like it was a story she was going to tell him. No, she didn't have guilt. Not for laying it all out to him, not for storming off. Glancing around the parking lot, she noted his car wasn't present and considered it a sign to go home.

Barely inside her single story East End ranch, Carly kicked off her shoes and let them land haphazardly on the black plastic tray she had by the door for dirty or wet footwear. She hadn't looked at them after leaving the edge of the river, but she presumed they should probably be considered filthy and likely needed a hose.

She grabbed the newspapers, journal and baseball cap from their seemingly permanent placement on the oversized armchair, dropped them on the couch, and flopped onto the now empty cushions—holding the beat up Brewers cap a little longer than necessary. The items, while they changed or were interchanged, were representative of the chair—the *pile chair*. The place he left whatever it was he was working on at the moment, and his damn thinking cap, always worn when he was writing up a new article. She didn't mind because it kept the couch free for them to share.

But tonight she didn't want to be on the couch. She wanted the tighter space of the armchair, so she could throw her legs over the side and curl up. She wanted to avoid thinking about the bullshit of life and the craziness of dead bodies long forgotten and coughed back up by the lake, so she grabbed the remote. Rather than turning it on and aimlessly flipping channels, she admitted she didn't know what she wanted to watch or if she even wanted the white noise to cover the buzzing in her head, afraid it would just blend and create a migraine, and tossed the remote over to the couch.

It was barely nine o'clock but she desperately wanted to be asleep, a limited leave of absence from reality. She glanced toward the kitchen. The empty bottle on the counter let her know she wasn't going to dull her way into a nice temporary coma, and she opted for a hot shower instead, hoping to wash the stink of dead bodies from her imagination and slough some of the pain that felt so very physical.

Halfway to the bathroom she changed her mind and turned into her bedroom. Carly fell, fully clothed, on top of her comforter. She lay there and thought about all the things she didn't want to think of, the bits she desperately wanted to forget, and the two new floaters who joined her memory bank of disgusting things she never expected to deal with as a cop.

CHAPTER THREE

Carly left her car in the public lot to the side of the municipal building, hoping to throw Parker off her location should he stop by the station. Rather than walking through the police station hallways to the other end of the building and the government offices housed there, she chose to walk around the station toward the doors that faced the large limestone and brick courthouse. No matter how often she found herself inside its walls, she would always find awe in the majestic county courthouse.

She remembered the first time she'd been inside it, frozen on those front steps, staring up at a building fit for forgotten gods, while the rest of her class scurried up the wide staircase and into the building. When she'd finally entered that day, she had been enthralled with the mild echo bouncing off the Bedford blue cut stone and Pavonazza marble of the interior. Carly chuckled to herself, as she heard the description in the voice of Ms. Rusch, her history teacher, from a tour she had memorized in eighth grade. The stair bannisters and upper railings were an intricate wrought iron painted white to match the marble around it. Ornate details in the doorways and the limestone crown moulding along the ceiling looked hundreds of years old, thousands, like something from an ancient Greek building. Even the oversized clock silently counting seconds on the wall above the elevator was stately.

There had been a beauty to the building she'd never seen before. The courthouse, the large Presbyterian Church across the street, and the Catholic Church down the block all seemed bigger than the town they were in, but it was the courthouse that kept her attention. It commanded respect. This is where laws were made and kept. She never dreamed she would work inside it, and was delighted when the city built a similarly styled building behind it, attached by a skywalk, and moved the police station and other government offices into it.

Today she wasn't going in the courthouse though. Today she was slipping into the back door and quietly taking the elevator to the fourth floor while she fondly remembered the first time she'd been in the courthouse. She didn't hear the elevator's telltale bell to announce the floor, but the doors opened and Parker stood in front of her.

She rolled her eyes and walked past him. To his credit, he followed without a word, and Carly wondered if he was building up the courage to say something specific or if maybe he'd finally figured out she didn't want to talk.

She pushed open the door to the medical examiner's office and stepped into the temperature-controlled office. Three desks with matching computers and multi-line telephones were littered with files, photos and other expected paraphernalia of the trade. While each had its own level of disarray or organization, dependent upon the desk, they were spaced evenly in the room and surrounded by black filing cabinets. At the right end of the room was a smaller wooden door with a frosted window. Stark black letters across the frost stated the position within: CHIEF MEDICAL EXAMINER.

Carly noted the three desks were empty and glanced at the wall clock. It was rare for them to all be out at once, so she imagined one or two of the deputy examiners was in the building. She cracked the chief's door and looked around. Pulling her phone from her pocket, she dialed the missing man.

"I'm downstairs, Carly," was followed by silence and she realized he'd tapped the phone on long enough to give her exactly what he knew she wanted and then hung up.

She sighed and spoke to the room, aiming the information at Parker without actually acknowledging him. "He's downstairs."

"Yuck."

Carly hated the morgue. Almost as much as she hated television and Hollywood for making it sound like cops and detectives, *and even reporters*—she thought as she sensed Parker following her back to the elevator—were okay with the sights and smells of the morgue. She hoped to never be okay with it.

They rode to the basement without a word, and Carly started to regret wishing for it, as silence echoed almost as loudly as heavy shoes did in the long basement hallways. She took a deep breath and opened the metal door, greeting the medical examiner with a smile she knew he wouldn't believe. "Morning, Donny."

"Cream's on the desk there. You'll want it." He looked over the edge of his glasses at her and nodded to indicate the location of the Vick's style menthol cream. She noticed his gray was becoming more and more silver and white, like he was starting to match his surroundings.

"That bad?" Parker mimicked Carly's actions, smearing a small amount of the cream under each nostril.

"Well, you know, dead bodies actually stink, Mr. Manning." Parker shot Carly a look at the formal use of his name and she recognized his stinging accusation that she had told Donny their current situation. She hadn't. Donny had just never liked nosy newsboys in his workroom. She smiled knowing the truth, and knowing the false assumption would make Parker crazy.

"Yeah…" Parker walked toward the metal table the medical examiner was hunched over.

"Well, to become *floaters* they have to fill up with

nasty gasses and fluids. And then we pull them out of the cold water and let them warm up—"

"Ew. Okay, I get it. Thanks for the cream." Parker shook his head.

"What's going on that you're still down *here*? Shouldn't it just be paperwork by now?"

"You would think that, wouldn't you?" Donny stood upright and finally faced them properly. Carly glanced without thinking at the body he was working on and quickly looked away. All she registered was it was the male victim, as there had been legs.

Carly swallowed her disgust and looked around the morgue. The floor was an immaculately laid, and often polished, white tile. The tables shone with an almost polished glimmer. Instruments on two trays, which reminded her of morbid cookie trays, were covered with a clean white cloth, and sat on the counter waiting for use. It was all very clean. Very orderly. Pristine. And smelled of nothing. She knew the smell of the room without the cream under her nose, which currently flavored the air a strong mint. She knew the cleaning chemicals used in the room were strong enough to counteract the stench of death, and the result was an almost neutral smell a novice wouldn't quite be able to pinpoint. She knew what it was. And she knew if he told her to mint-up, that meant today the room did not smell neutral, medicinal, or chemical. Today it smelled of death.

Two other bodies lay on cold metal beds, covered with crisp nonabsorbent sheets. A fourth gurney lay empty and exposed its truth, with the sheet folded at the ready near the end, and drainage slots through the center like some strange artistic ribs created by voids in the metal. Straps on the tables always freaked Carly out, like the dead had to be held down for some reason, and she had to remind herself it was to help move the bodies from table to drawer and back again. She saw a toe sticking out of one of the sheets and knew it wasn't her second victim, as it had been missing the bottom half.

"Did this guy come after us or did we butt in line?"

"Tell you the truth, I didn't even look at it. I came straight in for your floaters. What's the name on the tag there?"

Carly scrunched her nose and Parker, the closer of the two, leaned down and tilted his head to read the Sharpie on the four inch tag.

"It says Delcourt."

"Oh yeah. Nothing special there, just a standard autopsy." He shrugged, "He can take a number and wait. One of the deputies will do it as soon as they get down here." He glanced at the clock behind him and mumbled, "Actually, they should be down here already. Must have run for breakfast first."

Donny paused and made eye contact with each of them before a smile smeared its way across his face. "God you really hate it down here, don't you?"

"Yes, yes I do, Donny. And you know it. Now come on…" Carly tried to give him a stern look but was sure it appeared more like a child's tantrum.

"Alright, come here. And no, this isn't to torture you."

Carly and Parker stepped closer to the gurney and Donny poked at the flesh on the shoulder of the male corpse, his sleeve sliding up his wrist as he reached forward and the remnants of an old tattoo poked out past the cuff. Carly remembered Donny Meys had a past before going to medical school and becoming the ME. He'd been an ambulance driver in NYC *and* volunteer firefighter in his twenties, and while his accent was all but gone unless he got pissed off about something, the ink she'd seen had been indicative of his history. A two count of thought and Carly remembered without seeing the rest of the tattoo— it was a firehouse shield with a baseball bat across it, from his time on the engines and their municipal ball league.

"You see this? The way the muscle here is hardened but soggy? That's wrong. Like if you took a mummy and soaked it. The muscles won't get moist again, they won't absorb again, but they'll get slimy. That's what you've got here. If this was a floater, from the bottom, it would be waterlogged. It would be like meat you let marinate too long. Not like jerky dripping with water.

"And most of the organs are here, but again, hard. Like they were dried. Like this body was left out in the sun, and then buried, and then dug back up and dipped in water like an old tea bag."

"Well, I'm never drinking tea again." Parker curled a lip.

"Sorry, it's just... It's interesting. And floaters are never interesting. They're sad and horrible and chewed up and, well, this isn't." The lilt in his voice was almost childlike in his excitement.

"So you're saying this guy was sunk after he was left out? Why would that bitch of a lake float him up if he's a dry husk?"

"She wouldn't. That's the point. He's not a floater."

"He's not a —" Parker pulled his notebook from his pocket. "But why the nose cream?"

"Oh he still stinks pretty bad. They both do. So does Mr. Delcourt over there. But no, they're not traditional floaters. They may have floated, but they didn't float up from the bottom. Not this decade anyway."

"Ah shit, really? Homicide?"

"Yeah, but I wouldn't sweat it, Parker." Donny pulled

the body toward him carefully and folded down the shirt collar. "See this?"

"What? The old tag there?" She couldn't make out the writing on the tag and wondered what Donny was alluding to.

"They haven't made tags like this since the early 70s. And this shirt looks like it was new before the water got ahold of it. So I would make an educated guess, this guy died before 1980. This is a cold case, Carly, and you don't want anything to do with it. Last guy who played with a cold case from the lake wasn't seen again until retirement."

"But it's a murder."

"Maybe. Maybe not. Might actually have been natural causes. I couldn't find anything to lead me to believe there was foul play."

"So you think he's a dried out husk because he was properly buried? Is that why they seem more skeletal than most floaters? And if so, then how'd he end up in the water? On the shore? In my life?" She tried to hold back the frustration, but she knew if there weren't enough answers then the cold case would become active.

"Well, I'm not sure. But I can tell you he's white, and she's not." He nodded to the table next to her without the toe tag.

"What?" Parker's voice startled Carly, as she'd almost forgotten he was there.

"Well, she's Indian. As in Native American, not India Indian." He pointed at his forehead and Carly realized he was indicating a forehead bindi.

Carly ignored the inappropriate stereotyping and raised her eyebrows at the suggested racism, "Oh? Was interracial relationships with Indians a problem in the 70s?"

Donny chuckled, "I sometimes forget you're younger—the 70s don't seem that long ago to me." He walked over to the table holding the female half-body and pulled the sheet back, pointing at the buttons and stitches on the front of the shirt. "Yeah, they might have raised a close-minded eyebrow or two at the time, but that's not the issue here. Nor is it even possible in this situation, since she's been dead probably fifty or sixty years longer than him, if not more."

"Wait, what? How?" Carly leaned down and looked at the buttons, they were imperfect floral patterns with a handle style hole in the back. "Metal?"

"Glass actually. Early 20th century."

"Which is why she's in worse shape than him?"

Donny shrugged, "Like I said, it's interesting." Donny pulled the sheet back up. "I'm going to do some dating tests and see if I can't pinpoint their years of death. I've already put a call in to the college. I'll have Erin come do a sketch after we put some depth markers on the skulls and see if we can't get a better idea of what these two might have looked like before death. And of course, you said you've got Gunderson searching missing persons. If you put him in the right decades it might speed things up. But still, you do not want a cold case file. Remember that."

"I know, but you also know I can't just let shit go, either." She didn't see Parker nodding in agreement, as her phone rang and she grabbed it as a lovely distraction. "Greene." She saw both men watching her as she listened to Babybird's words and knew they were paying attention to the expression she had to be making. "Okay. On my way."

She pocketed the phone and looked at Donny, "Years apart or not, they're not alone this thaw. We got another floater, Donny."

"I'll drive." He pulled the white apron from the front of him and tossed it into the hamper.

"Good, 'cos I'm *not* putting one of them in my car."

"No worries. Help me wheel these two back into the freezer." Donny laughed and looked at Parker, "Kick that wheel brake off and follow me. Carly, open the door for us?"

• • • • •

The three of them found the officers on the east side of the bridge, further downstream from the first discovery. The body lay face down at Mikey Gunderson's feet. The young officer was sitting on the slope of the bank with a tire iron in his hand, two other officers Carly didn't recognize standing next to him.

"Babybird?" She called out to him and saw the other officers smirk. He turned back to her and stood, walking up to meet her halfway.

"This is fucking gross, Detective Greene."

"Oh Christ, call me *Carly*. You know that."

"Fine. *Carly*, it's fucking gross." He took a deep breath. "Those two answered the call from the gas station attendant. Got here and froze. They called me because they heard about yesterday. I get here and the body is out a couple feet, snagged on a branch." He held up the tire iron, "I had to use *something* to hook the fucking thing and pull it to shore. The iron went right through the ribs like they were crackers. I finally got a grip on it and what do I see as I'm pulling it in? A whole shit ton of little fish down there following their lunch to shore. Gross." He looked from Parker to the men, pausing on Donny, "How do you deal with this?"

"Easy, son. Just remember it's someone's kid or spouse,

and was a person. No matter how gross it is, someone out there needs closure on it." Donny pulled gloves from his pocket and stretched them over his hands as he walked toward the body.

"You did good, Mikey." Carly looked up at the other two. "You guys can head back, we don't need you."

"No wait, please." Donny called from the body. "They can help us bag it in a few."

The officers both made faces of disgust and sighed.

"You find anything on the missing persons?" Carly tried to distract Mikey.

"Nah, and I went through that crap until well after midnight."

"Well, Donny thinks they're older bodies. As in *decades* from being fresh. So once he ages them properly, we'll have you look again in the right era at least."

"Decades? They that old?"

Carly nodded and put a hand out to stop Parker from walking toward Donny, like a mother stopping a kid in the passenger seat from a sudden brake. "No. You let him work. You let us work. You take notes from back here." She looked between them, "Why don't you ask Officer Gunderson here some background and filler questions for your write-up." She smiled to herself for occupying both of them and walked over to the body and Donny.

"Carly, look at this." She hadn't thought she'd been that noisy on the slick ground, but Donny seemed to sense when she was close enough to speak directly to her.

She squatted down, "Look at what?"

"Well, the water is high as hell this year because of the fast thaw. High water rushes more, has swirls and ebbs and currents, right?"

"Yeah," Carly looked to the shoreline and noted it was at *least* five feet higher up the bank than it should be, probably more but she was unfamiliar with this particular shoreline.

"That brings in bigger fish, but these marks are all small. Small and circular, with strange lashes that don't really seem like fish marks." Donny picked at the cloth on the well-chewed arm and shrugged.

"Like maybe she scrapped along a barbed wire fence or something upstream?"

"No. That's the thing, the slashes are bloodless wounds. I mean, there's no blood now, obviously, because she's been soaking. But some of these wounds were made while she was alive, not postmortem. It's…"

"She's been soaking? So this one *is* a floater?"

"Oh, she floated. And she's not old. This is fresh. This is definitely this winter. Look at her clothes, though. No jacket. You don't fuck with this lake anywhere near freeze or thaw without a jacket."

"There's always someone in the bunch who doesn't think it's as cold as it real—" Carly glanced back at the river and cocked her head at the water, as if mimicking a confused dog. She stood up and slowly raised her hand in front of her to point like a one-armed mummy. "What. Is. That?" Each word was punctuated with a pause and a palpable fear of the next word.

Donny stood and turned around toward the river. Parker and Gunderson were suddenly next to her.

"What? Where?" Gunderson squinted toward the water.

"There." She was still pointing, her arm frozen in the air. "Tell me those are logs…" Three dark shapes bobbed in the water, lazily following the current pushing them from under the bridge, from upstream.

"They're… not." Donny spoke the same time as Parker.

"Oh my god." Parker swallowed loudly.

The three of them turned as one to look upstream.

Mikey gasped recognition as the coffin floating nearest the shoreline veered on a current and lodged itself against a large fallen tree sticking out into the water, the wood of the ancient casket cracking loudly and threatening to spill its contents.

Carly broke the silence and voiced what the others were thinking, "The cemetery!"

CHAPTER FOUR

They had hopped into the cars and sped the six blocks west to the cemetery—Carly and Donny in his vehicle, while Parker tagged along with Officer Gunderson rather than being a third wheel in the cramped front seat of the meat wagon.

There are three kinds of cemeteries in the world. The forgotten roadside graves, which naturally look haunted, with its crooked stones and wooden barricades begging to be crossed. The huge stately city cemeteries with iron gates and plots like tiny castles all crowded into borrowed land. And the clean, low-key, almost *boring* in their organization graveyards, which Carly referred to as suburbia for the dead. This particular graveyard was the third kind.

Locals referred to this one as the Nemadji Cemetery because of its proximity to the river, but it was *technically* the St. Francis Cemetery, owned and maintained by the Catholic church of the same name in East End. It was clean and quiet, and was usually empty, as it sat on a side road travelled only by those who lived in the neighborhood before the cemetery or those going to work in the fields of Enbridge Energy down the road. The cemetery itself was neither country nor city, sitting where it did, in a strange placement between town and the swampland banks of the river. The cemetery was obviously there first. Houses and businesses and the future came later.

Carly had spent a lot of time in this graveyard as a child, having lived less than a mile away and being free on her bike to roam East End during summer break. She had walked through the stones, making up stories of the lives left behind by the names she could read, and often deciding how they so tragically or naturally ended up here.

As they turned onto the single lane paved path, which split the graveyard in two, Donny brought the car to a stop, pausing at the unmarked, ungated entrance. Carly looked for things out of place but saw nothing to explain the coffins. No large equipment, no active funeral. To the left of what passed for a one-way road through the stones was the youth section, closest to the road, where the rows were dotted with several lamb and angel statues. The stones themselves in this section were much like those they marked, smaller. She noted they were generally brighter if not white, and were topped with trinkets, toys, and other small items of mourning, loss and memory. Carly remembered the time she'd found several lamb statues broken and sat weeping, unable to understand why someone would vandalize a child's grave.

Behind the youth section, the stones looked darker. Carly knew the visual illusion was less about the color of the stones being in contrast to the lighter marble of the youth section, and more due to the area being an older portion of the cemetery. The markers in the back were made up of mostly limestone, which over time darkened, welcoming moss and decay much quicker than other stones. A large rock monument with a plague on it was visible from the road, and though she couldn't make out the words from there, she knew it was a monument to the founders and first settlers who were buried in the overgrown corner at the very back of the older section. She and every teenager to ever enter this cemetery had wondered how many stones were lost to the shadows of untrimmed brambles and unchecked saplings taking root and providing a dank canopy. How many stones were covered in moss? How many had sunken into the moist land near the river?

To the right was the more modern general section,

the area Carly thought of as a gated community, complete with neighborhood watchdogs and a homeowner's association making sure the flowers were placed *just so* and the grass was mowed to the perfect height. While there was obvious order and planning of the plots, the section still had some distinction among the rows with an array of stones, statues and benches—an overall strange display of funeral evolution, in both style and size if you scanned it as a whole. To Carly, this was the main graveyard and the only area she'd ever attended a funeral. She found, even as an adult, the larger than life-size statues gave her the creeps and made the cleaner, newer section somehow more disturbing than the sections begging for a foggy night and careful of easily scared teenagers.

Except in the far back corner, where there was only sadness and a strange unassociated guilt she couldn't explain. She glanced at the wooden sign. She could make out where the tree line began to slope down toward the river. She knew the area was considered the Native American section, where over two hundred bodies—

"Donny, the Indian section in the back." She flicked a finger to indicate the area she referred to. "Didn't you say the female on the table was old and Native?"

He nodded and eased the car forward, going straight down the path toward the river rather than following the curving one-way avenue through the stones. He drove slowly, deliberately, as he swerved to avoid large potholes filled with water and questionable mud ruts.

"Were there even coffins involved in that? I mean, do you know the history?" Carly stared at the area as if she expected something to happen.

"Enough, yes. What I've heard over the years from the tribe members or gossip." Donny pulled the car to a stop on the top of the downward slope where the pavement became a dirt path, which led to a muddy looking parking area and the river itself. "We should probably walk from here." He nodded to the high water and red clay puddles below.

"Yeah." Carly agreed and stepped out of the car.

Most of the graves were behind them from this vantage point. Carly looked over the top of the roof past Donny to see the large rock Founders' Monument up close. As she turned around, slowly scanning from the oldest section to the portion of the river visible at the bottom of the dirt road, and continuing on to the back of the modern area. Distinctly different from the clean, plainly laid out neat rows of marble and granite, a thin line of trees and large bushes marked an unofficial perimeter for the graves at the back—the area where there were actually stones for the Chippewa who were buried here *properly*. She noted fallen trees—mixed in with the twisted knots of branches and trimmings—at the back edge of the cemetery, where the thin perimeter of trees became a small copse separating the dead from the river.

She heard the doors of the other car close and turned to face Mikey and Parker.

"I'm going to head over that way, you two check this end." Carly nodded at the wooden sign marking the Indian burial area. She couldn't refer to it as a burial ground, not a proper one anyway. She knew enough to know there were no headstones of granite, marble or even wood there. There were no small mound houses marking graves. There was no rice and tobacco offerings left at any tomb of sorts. Not like those she'd seen near the Bad River reservation by Ashland. Not even like the ones still out on Wisconsin Point—leftovers from those who were moved here.

Moved, she thought. More like dumped.

As she crossed the grass and passed through the small pointless barrier of small pines, Carly recalled what she knew of the displacement of the Indians she was currently marching toward.

Originally part of a settlement on Wisconsin Point, over one hundred and eighty graves were moved from the point to this graveyard in 1918 to make way for some business. The land on the point turned out to be not solid for building and the business plan was scraped, but not before almost two hundred sacred native bodies were unceremoniously dumped on the side of the hill between the Catholic graveyard and the river. She remembered something about them being loaded onto a barge, sent upriver, dumped and barely covered—as if not being Catholic meant they weren't worthy of respect on this sacred ground. It was all bullshit, and disrespectful as hell in her mind, and she truly hoped she wouldn't find what she feared waiting for her down the slope beyond the wooden sign.

"Did you hear me?" Donny's longer stride had negated her quick steps.

"Sorry." She hadn't even heard him talking while she'd been seething about history that didn't involve her.

"I said there were no coffins. Not that I'm aware of. They brought those folks and dumped them in a mass grave. Loose bodies could be coming from there, but the floating coffins, the wood boards from yesterday, those would be—."

"You were saying?" Carly stopped dead in her tracks at the wooden sign.

Beyond it, the water had raised enough to not only wash away part of the hillside and expose several of the remains buried there, but it had also caused the boards placed over the bodies to break loose. One of the boards no longer covering the remains had tried to float away but clung to the red clay it had called home, swaying in the current while it waited for something to dislodge it. At least three other boards were visibly missing.

A casual glance would make one believe random sticks were poking out of the dirt and clay at a variety of angles. Only if you were looking for bones would you even recognize them as such. Mud and streaks of dried clay mottled the straight lengths of gray bones. Darker patches stained the knobs near the knuckles, balls and joints, where the padding of cartilage had long rotted away and connective tendons had dried into something almost like jerky or leather, in both texture and color. Dogwoods, that's what they reminded Carly of, the dogwood logs her father used to gather on camping trips. Gray brittle sticks, from twigs for kindling to thicker branches for the fire logs themselves—had she known then what she knew now, the campfire would have been viewed in a much more morbid light.

Carly could make out several bones, and from the placement was trying to decide how many bodies they belonged to. She pointed as she counted out loud to Donny, "That's a leg over there and an arm, I think they're the same body. Another arm there makes two. Another arm, or is that a leg, I can't see the end, that's three. And is that… Donny, is that a rib cage?"

"I believe it is, yes. I'll need to get the boys and go down there and see what kind of damage has been done to the mass grave—"

"You mean dumping ground?"

"Yeah, that. But I don't know if this is cemetery land or Ojibwa land. I'm not even sure if I have jurisdiction here."

"Would it be Bad River or Red Cliff?"

"Neither, it's actually Fond du Lac I think."

"Really? Duluth? Shit, that crosses borders and makes all kinds of things messy."

"That's why I was asking earlier if you knew the history. The original settlement and graves out on the point were the Fond du Lac tribe. They eventually moved west, into Duluth, Cloquet, etcetera." Donny pointed out two more skeletal limbs, one with a bit of cloth still clinging to the memory of decency. "Superior is kind of a weird dead zone where the bands all meet but no one really claims land here anymore. I mean, there are stragglers from the original settlement out on the point, I know a neighborhood in Allouez has descendants, but most moved on to Minnesota as the Madeline bands of Red Cliff and Bad River spread this way more."

"How do you know more than me about this? I grew up here. Sorta. You're from New York."

"True, but I have a chief deputy and two lesser deputies that are local. And this," he pointed down the hill at the exposed mass grave, mud and dirt and years worth of weeds and reeds washing away in the high water, "This is death, Carly. This is what my guys live to talk about, to explore. When they find out this has happened out here, I won't even have to beg them for overtime. They'll camp out until we kick them out."

"I guess I never thought of that. Gross as I find all of this, it's what you—"

"Guys!" Mikey's high-pitched cry sounded like pain, but Carly knew it was inexperienced panic she was hearing.

"Hang on. I'll be right back." She held a finger up at Donny and took off.

Jogging halfway back to the car, Carly met a wide-eyed Parker who simply pointed down the hill toward Mikey.

The young officer was bent over, hanging out above the water, both his hands white-knuckled as they gripped the edge of a coffin attempting to float away.

"What the hell?"

"There." Parker pointed to the ground and Carly saw the flat, mostly overgrown stones at the edge of the hill. Approximately five feet down the hill the water, which would normally be another four feet below that, lapped at the dirt and clay, causing an erosion tunnel and leaving a lip of barely sustainable turf. She saw the twin streaks torn through the grass where Mikey had attempted to stand and his weight had not only dropped him and the false canopy, but he had knocked the coffin loose from whatever had been holding it.

"Jesus." She glanced back at Donny who shrugged.

"Can you crawl down there and give him a hand back up? Tell him to let go of it if he has to. We'll just have to fetch that coffin with the rest of them downstream for now."

Parker nodded frantically and inched his way down to Mikey. Carly dragged a foot across the flat stone Parker had pointed out, "1868..." She took a lunging step to her right and poked at the ground until she located another. Calculating the distance between them and the space between the rows, "Jesus... there could be as many as twenty close enough for erosion."

She ran back to Donny's position. "Without climbing down, what can you see?"

"I see erosion, bad erosion. We're going to have some pissed off Natives if this doesn't get taken care of properly."

"How many bodies do you think—"

"Carly, I haven't the slightest clue how they were stacked or exactly where along the hillside. The exposed we can see could be the top of the pile, or just the side of it and it goes off that way more. And I seriously doubt anyone who was involved with the actual movement of these bodies is still alive."

"Shit. Okay. We need more bodies here. Live bodies. Let's get back up, call your boys, and reconvene."

She turned and headed back to the road, Donny's footsteps told her he followed. Parker and Mikey—the entire left side of him covered in the stain of wet red clay, a stark contrast to the pale of his blood drained face— stood by the car. She shook her head, her mind spinning a hundred directions.

This is not detective work. This is a whole lot of someone else's problem.

She turned to Donny, "How close do you suppose they were buried to the hillside?"

He glanced at the area and shrugged, "Maybe they weren't. How many times have we had a bad thaw like this over the years? Maybe the river grew over the cemetery rather than the other way around."

"Mikey, from down there, what could you see?"

"That I'd need a boat."

She squinted but held her tongue, deciding he hadn't meant that to sound nearly as snarky as it had. "And maybe I'll make you my bitch on this one." She smiled and he nodded a polite acquiescence. He was a good grunt, a hard worker, but he also had a decent sense of humor, which might come in handy on this one.

Glancing over her shoulder, toward the front of the cemetery, Carly spotted the small brick building which served as the caretaker's hut. No longer used for overnight vigils under the guise of security, it now housed what represented an office for paperwork and a tool closet for the workers. She didn't imagine it was a full-time job and saw no vehicles or movement. Beyond the caretaker's building, hidden in the edge of the woods just out of sight of the casual funeral attendee, was a pile of discarded offerings—both dead and fake flowers, as well as empty containers, tossed haphazardly and looking not unlike a junk yard pile of faded colors and waterlogged garbage. She wondered if that would get buried, burned or just bagged and thrown away when no one was looking. It seemed cruel to her for it to just be there in the open, exposing just how disposable humans are, even after they're dead.

"Mikey, call the church and get someone out here who knows what's what back here."

He nodded and pulled his cell out as he leaned against the car, the color finally starting to return to his face.

"You call your boys. I'll call the chief." She turned to Parker, "Could you possibly *not* call anyone yet? Can you keep this quiet until we have a bit of a grip on it?"

He nodded at her words but his eyes were locked on the river.

• • • • •

Four medical examiners carefully watched their footing on the mass burial hill, attempting to place markers for bodies. All they could do at the moment was tag what they could see, while waiting to hear from the tribe about whether or not they were allowed to extract the bodies— yet again. Without meaning disrespect, but as Donny had said to the chief of police, talking over Carly's shoulder and into her phone, "we need a head count. Gotta know how many had gone floating down river."

Three rowboats with small engines were in the river, two cops in each. One busily attempted to secure a net across the river to catch anything else trying to float away.

The other two were puttering along the shoreline taking notes and pictures and calling back up to those on shore with information and suggestions.

The chief sat in his oversized Expedition and talked to Carly through the window.

"You're point on this. You started it, you finish it. We don't have a whole lot going on right now and you've got a good face and attitude for the delicate nature of this problem."

"You mean you need a girl to calm down the survivors of our floating cemetery?"

"Not to put too fine a point on it… but yeah. You okay with that?"

She didn't believe she had a choice, whether he made it sound like she did or not. "How long is Sparkman gone for trial?"

"Only until tomorrow, trial went short. Why? What do you want with Ben?"

"Nothing, but I want to keep Babybird on this with me."

"Babybird. You really have to stop calling him that. He'll never tell you, but he really does hate it."

She made a genuine face of surprise and nodded, glancing over to the young officer. She made a mental note to call him by his first name, and maybe he'd start using hers. No need for formality within the department, especially when he worked with Sparky.

"But yeah, you can keep Gunderson. Hell, you can have Sparkman when he gets back tomorrow. Beyond that, if you need bodies after we get a grip on this out here, let me know. I'm sure we can give you some shift boys."

"How about Lucas? It'd be good for him."

"He being a dick to you again?" The chief gave her a

knowing look.

"I'm here aren't I? He knows I hate the floaters and yet he went directly for me."

"He does know that, but in truth, you were on deck for next incident. The other five are on active cases. You just wrapped the Sanders thing last week and were doing nothing but stalk the hot sheets and avoiding Parker. Plus Lucas isn't street, he's chair, and would just get in your way and piss you off."

"Fine. It's mine. But thanks for offering other help. Ben and Mikey will be great assets, maybe get this wrapped up quickly." She watched three uniforms at the edge of the hill. They were securing rope at each marker and tossing the other end down to be secured below, by the boys in the rowboats. The hope was to mark those already gone floating for easier body identification, and keep the others from so easily sliding out of the mud wall the banks had become.

"Don't thank me. I'm pretty sure you're still going to hate this." He nodded toward Parker, helping the cops rather than taking pictures. "You guys okay yet?"

"You don't pay me enough for us to have that conversation." She looked down and hoped he hadn't seen the flash of pain in her eyes.

He laughed, "Understood. Do I need to have him removed?"

"Nah, he's fine. Though I'm going to have to put him behind the rope line when the others figure it out and come out, with their vans and microphones and causes they know nothing about to claim disrespect of Indian burial grounds and poor city planning."

The chief started his SUV, "You got this."

"Hope so." She turned and walked toward Parker, preparing to forewarn him of his future on the other side of the rope line. A long black ripple rolled through the water and knocked one of the rowboats, almost tossing the officer at the bow over the edge. She heard him scream in shock and watched him curse his pilot.

"What the fuck was that?"

"It wasn't me!" The pilot looked at the dirty water of the Nemadji, the red-brown clay-dyed water was completely opaque. "Something hit us."

"Probably just a sturgeon," the officer from the other boat yelled over. "We gotta be disturbing them being in the river this time of year."

"Awesome. Dead bodies *and* big ugly fish." Carly spoke under her breath as she came to a halt next to Parker.

CHAPTER FIVE

Rob Ullman and Seth Warrick had been best friends since the fifth grade. They'd failed ninth grade together and almost done eleventh grade twice together, but made it through by the skin of their teeth. They were tighter than kin, working together, playing together—they'd even lived together a short time.

And they'd been on the mouth of the Nemadji in their matching red flannel shirts since just before sunrise, patiently waiting for daybreak and the early morning mist they knew made the fish bite so well. The second Thursday in May meant if you could find open water, you could fish. All breeds were open for season except the sturgeon, which could only be caught during September and no casual fisherman was interested in those anyway. Rob and Seth were looking for early season small mouth, as Rob swore the meat was better before the water warmed up.

"It's firm, like fake titties." He took a bite of the peanut butter and jelly on white bread he'd packed for lunch but was eating well ahead of schedule.

Seth shook his head, tearing open a small bag of chips. "You ain't never felt a fake titty in your life. Hells, you've been with Ash since she got pregnant our senior year. And you'll be with her until she kills you, 'cos you ain't got it in you to ever leave."

"Can't. Even if I wanted. Her dad went and cosigned on the house and my truck, and I ain't losing my truck." He looked at the dirt road past the weeds they had pushed the boat thru and saw his pride and joy—a red S10 sitting there with its doors hanging open.

"Asshole. You leave the doors like that?"

"I had to. I couldn't stand the stink anymore."

"Fuck you, it don't stink that bad." Rob stepped

from the boat into the shallows of weeds where they'd been fishing since dawn, waiting to head upstream for the afternoon when the sun got a little higher and drove the fish to the deeper cooler water of the river. The water was high, but still well below his waders in the inlet just outside the mouth of the river by the grain elevators— technically considered the shallows during thaw, there normally wasn't more than a couple inches of swamp water in this area due to sandbars.

"It don't fucking stink that bad." He mumbled to himself as he trudged through the tall combination of reeds, pussy willows and cattails.

The Saturday before, opening weekend for bass on the tributaries, Seth had gotten chicken livers on sale at the grocery store. It sounded like a good idea for bait, and the channel cats seem to really like it. But when Rob knocked the container off the seat and spilled chicken livers and the organ flavored juices they had been stewing in, the carpet of his truck and the cushion of the seat were officially disgusting. He scraped the chunks back into the container and soaked up what he could with an old T-shirt he pulled from under the seat, and they fished until dark. The tradition of opening weekend meant they had to stop out at Grumpy's Tavern and tell tales of the fish they couldn't prove they'd caught. By the time he'd dropped Seth at home and stumbled into his one-level ranch a block shy of the wrong side of the tracks, he'd forgotten about the chicken livers. The Old Milwaukee hangover had kept him on the couch the next day while the livers cooked in the heat of an unusual spring sun. He'd tried a hose, bleach, and even vinegar throughout the week to no avail. Not only was the smell still evident, being organ meat just made it smell like death had its own hangover.

Rob reached the truck and slammed the door shut. "I mean, it stinks, but it's getting better." He refused to admit even to himself the smell was what caused him to throw up the next time he got in. He claimed the flu, bad food, anything but the fact a *smell* could be so bad he would actually vomit.

He went around the other side and shut the passenger door after rolling the window down. He could always air it out a little...

Seth's scream stopped Rob's monologue of excuses and he darted back around the truck to the riverside.

"Seth?" He called back, his eyes focusing on his friend in time to see what looked like a huge black snake pulling Seth from the boat. "What the fuck?!" Seth's wide eyes disappeared on the other side of the boat and a large splash let Rob know his friend had gone under water against his will.

Rob pushed his way through the weeds faster than anyone would have guessed his overweight diabetic body was capable of moving. "Seth!" He called again as he neared the boat. *Couldn't be a snake. Not that big. And no way a sturgeon grabs a person. No way.*

The black snake shot out of the water and slapped down on the boat, breaking through the side of the hull like a karate master on a pile of boards. Another snake skimmed across the water toward Rob, flicking haphazardly at the noises he was making in the water. Rob froze. *Those are not snakes. Those are... they're... what the hell are those?*

Again the tentacle rose and slapped near him and he flinched but remained frozen.

Maybe it can't see me. Maybe if I don't move—

The tentacle rose again, this time it was close enough for Rob to see the detail. The black meat waving in front of him hypnotically reminded him of a catfish—not scaled like a normal fish and not slick like a snake, but rather, the fine sandpaper of what his uncle had always called water-flesh, easier to clean than scales. The smooth skin and deep rich black of the thing made him think of leeches, the water making it shine like a perfectly polished military shoe.

Leech? No way. Leeches don't get this big. Oh god. Eels? Do we have lampreys this fucking big in here? He gasped at the thought.

The five-foot length of black flinched at the sound and turned. Flaps that looked useless dotted the length of the tentacle, strange wrinkles of flesh that made no sense to him. No sense until they flexed, widening like Rob's eyes as his expression changed from confusion to surprise, and fear. They became rigid and round and when it snapped forward with purpose, it found purchase on his shoulder.

The tentacle wrapped up over his shoulder like a buddy's hand slapping you for a job well done and the grip of each of those rigid round bits of flesh tightened. He could feel the pressure through his heavy flannel and beat up Country Jam concert shirt. The tentacle tugged him off balance and he went down, but before he could even make a splash, the other tentacle came up and grabbed his other shoulder. Together, they slapped him face-first into the water and pulled him from shore. Rob snapped out of it and began screaming a moment too late. His last breath was filled with Lake Superior's rancid swamp water in the weedy bay.

CHAPTER SIX

It had been a long day, and worn out as Carly was, the night offered no rest. Tossing and turning all night, her head filled with nightmares of floating coffins, the dead swimming up to boats, and even zombies walking out of the water toward a beach full of sunbathers, made for a very tired Carly slumping on the rolling chair next to the gurney Donny stood next to.

"You look like hell."

"I feel it."

"Well, I didn't get much sleep either, if that makes you feel better."

She looked up and saw Donny's eyes looked like hers felt. *A shot or three, and a nap, sound perfect right now*, she thought, *and it's not even noon yet.*

"So, after cataloging what we could move, I'm back here and I've got a deputy examiner at the cemetery. The other two are lost in paperwork and bummed they pulled long straws. Can you believe the three of them were fighting over who got to hang out at the graveyard?"

"Not really, no. Not after what you said about this being the kind of thing they'd really get into." She raised an eyebrow at him, "Which is still bizarre. Even though I understand where y'all are coming from. Wait, *hang out*? Why is anybody *hanging out* at the cemetery?"

"The rule is *if we can't move the body to a secure location, an examiner will stay with it until it is claimed.* Stupid as hell considering it's a graveyard, and there are already two cops sitting there in a squad watching the tape line so no reporters or snoopy teenagers go poking around. But rules is rules and if we don't follow them to the letter, somewhere somehow this will bite us in the ass."

"I suppose. No different than police protocol and

creating inadmissible evidence or tainted crime scenes."

"Exactly. So where are we with the Indians?" Donny spoke as he returned his attention to the woman on the metal table in front of him. Leaning in close, he moved cloth and tissue carefully as he examined the body.

"We are officially nowhere. You wouldn't believe how hard it is to get anyone's permission to do anything. You know the man I spoke to on the phone actually said, *Well good, I'm glad they're breaking free. The current will bring them right back to the point where they belong.* Seriously, that was his actual response."

"Was that the chief?"

"Nah, just whoever answered the phone."

"You may have to go up to the res in Cloquet…"

"Yeah, I know. I've got a few more numbers to call and the guy *did* say if I went out to the Allouez band that they could make local decisions. Allouez band? You know anything of this? Am I missing something?"

"It's not a reservation or even openly tribal if you're not part of the neighborhood, so no, you wouldn't be aware. Unlike out in Ashland, where the Bad River res has its own police and social services, this is literally just a dead end street where the Fond du Lac's from the point—those who didn't move on to Minnesota anyway—settled when they chose to stay behind. I guess they had some duty to the remaining burial sites on the point or something. I'm not positive why they stayed, but they are there. I've had to do a couple autopsies to determine medical or medicinal deaths."

"Medicinal? What, like Peyote?"

"Nah, nothing quite so exotic. More like, heart attack versus liver failure due to alcohol abuse." He looked at her over the top of his glasses. It was an expression and pose she was used to from him.

"Oh. I see. Bad drinkers?"

"Not anything more than the white folk around here. But when the survivors know and admit the problem, an autopsy becomes necessary for paperwork so official cause of death is a bit more than just *natural causes*."

"You got a number for someone out there? The guy on the phone was less than helpful."

"Maybe in a file somewhere. Probably easier just to go on out. You'll actually know exactly what houses from the décor and signs and such. They're a proud people." He gave her a very serious glance. "Just past President's Liquor, go left on 39th and then right on Itasca. The remainders of the tribe are all housed from about 41st all the way to the bay—remember, that's not actually Lake Superior proper right there, it's Allouez Bay. And directly across from that area is the Wisconsin Point burial grounds."

"Bays, inlets, whatever. You know I call it all *the beast*—Lake Superior."

"Beast is a good word for her." He snickered, "A beauty of a beast."

She shook her head at him but smiled at the bad pun. "You got a name at least?"

"Yeah, but you can't laugh. Especially out there."

She furrowed her brows, confused at the request. "What do you mean? Is it like Chief Flying Eagles or something? I know they use those names. Remember I come from Ashland. I'm used to the res. Plus I'm like one-sixteenth Chippewa or something. Just enough to take the beading class back in grade school. A thirty-second maybe? But mostly, I'm not rude."

"Okay then, it's Granny Two Fingers you'll want to talk to then. She always seemed to be the one everyone turned to for the final answer on anything when I've been out that way. They even brought her in with them for paperwork once. She never spoke, but they looked at her like she was talking to them telepathically before they answered or signed anything."

"Granny, eh? A matriarch. I like it." She stood and stretched. "I suppose I might as well head that way and see which direction they lead me."

"Um, Carly. Before you do that." He stood up suddenly, pulling back from the body in front of him. "This one was never buried. Our actual floater from yesterday."

Donny gave her a sympathetic look she was all too familiar with.

"Homicide." She sighed.

"Actually, I'm not sure."

"What? Why?"

He motioned her to come closer. "I really wanted to assume she was part of the Nemadji nightmare—."

"Is that what we're calling it?"

"Would you prefer the Great Graveyard Escape?"

She huffed half a laugh, "No. Continue." She shook her head and appreciated his attempt to beat the media to a catchy name for the horrible events.

"Well, like I said, at first I wanted her to be part of the… nightmare. A newer coffin that broke apart, or something. *Maybe*. Because a floater amongst all that was just too much of a coincidence. But her clothes caught my attention right away on the river bank, remember? These are not funeral clothes. I don't care how poor you are, you're dressed better than this for your own funeral. A long sleeve shirt, jeans, what I presume was a *pair* of winter boots." He pointed with his forceps as he spoke, stopping on the single boot.

"I see what you mean. And she's, um…" Carly glanced at the five coffins currently sitting on stands rather than tables, waiting their turn to be cataloged. "Fleshier? Is that how you would say it?"

"Good a term as any, I suppose. And yes, she is. But if you look here." He pointed to the wound on her neck and a similar wound on her arm. "That's not fish bites. Like I started to say at the scene yesterday. This was something else."

"Like a sturgeon or something?"

"Maybe. I'm going to look at the wounds under the microscope and get some photos."

"Any I.D. on her?"

"Jesus. You know in the crazy of coffins and bodies and Native American mass graves, I…" He patted the front pockets of the corpse's jeans and raised an eyebrow. Using only his thumb and index finger to reach in and retrieve the item, he pulled out a small pouch and set it in a metal pan on the tray next to him. Carly watched as he slid his hands underneath the soggy body—she presumed in lieu of flipping it over only to turn it back again—and checked the back pockets before shaking his head.

"Evidence?" He held up the pouch with his gloved hand.

"Fingerprints would be ruined by water and time so, no. No worries. What is that?"

"It's supposed to be a coin purse, but it's stiff. I can feel that. And I'd be willing to bet…" He unzipped it and pulled free a perfectly preserved laminated driver's license. "Yup, just like my girls. Both of my daughters hate purses. They carry little pouches like this with a driver's license, credit card and cash and that's it. I think everything else they need nowadays is on their phones."

Carly nodded, thinking of her own version of a wallet in lieu of a purse—a hard credit card holder with three slots for cards and a clip for cash—*because a purse on this job is just silly.*

He held out the license to her and Carly grimaced at the sludge on it. "Oh shit, sorry." He turned and ran the license under warm water in the sink, wiping it with a stiff paper towel from the stack on the counter and turned back to Carly. "Juliet Germain. Cute girl."

"Shit. No." Carly grabbed the I.D. and checked the address, *Billings Park*. "Damn it. I know her. Well, knew her. Not personally or anything, but she came in a few times looking for non-official help with her husband. He beat the crap out of her but she was too afraid to press charges. Damn it."

"These aren't knife wounds, Carly." She understood his suggestion that she thought it was murder. She still did, just maybe not a knife.

"I still gotta bring the husband in. Because of the history and such. Wow, I didn't even recognize her... Hang on, I'll be back." Carly walked out of the office, Juliet's driver's license still in her hand. She turned left and started walking toward the elevators but stopped at the bench opposite the silver doors. She didn't feel like going up to the precinct and getting caught up in all this. She still had to go out to Allouez. She pulled her phone from her pocket and dialed Mikey.

"Gunderson."

"Hey Babybir— Mikey. Got a task for you."

"Sure. Whatcha need?"

"The woman from the shore yesterday is a local. An abused spouse but not dead that I ever heard of. Pull her record and see what info you can find. She was in a couple times last year due to beatings. Bring me the file downstairs and then head over to his house—" Carly pulled the phone away and looked at the time on it. "Or his job, wherever he may be, and bring him in. We're going to have to question him on this."

"No problem. I'll do it now."

"Thanks Mikey. Her name is Juliet Germain, the husband was William, *Bill*, if I remember correctly. See you in a few."

CHAPTER SEVEN

Carly closed her eyes and waited on the bench for the young officer. She didn't expect it would take him more than ten minutes and she could use the quiet. Five coffins so far, two bodies without coffins on the shore one day, another the next day that turns out to be a floater. A lot of work for the medical examiners, and a lot of copy for the journalists—

Hmmm, I wonder if Parker is out at the cemetery. She could just imagine him with his laptop in the car, typing away on two different versions of the same story. He was always prepared for Saul's wishy-washy attitude, never knowing if his editor wanted the serious spin or the social conscious twist on any given story.

The elevator dinged and opened, revealing Mikey holding a blue binder.

"That was fast."

"I do what I can." He smiled and handed over the binder before pushing the L button to return to the floor above. "I was literally just waiting for orders from you. Chief said I'm your bitch on this, so I'm off desk and street. Heading over to find the husband now."

She nodded and opened the folder as the doors closed and the hallway returned to silence. Refreshing her memory on the case she'd been helpless to do anything with unless the wife actually pressed charges, she flipped through the pages. She only skimmed the forms and reports containing her own handwriting or signature, but took her time on the other documents. And then she came to the last page. The final entry. The missing person's report.

"Oh hell." She looked up at the ceiling but couldn't find the words to express her disgust at the husband. *It's a good thing Mikey's coming for you and not me, Mr. wife-beater.*

"Wait wait wait… what the hell?" She started speaking out loud to herself as she blinked and went back a paragraph. "*Crap.*"

She pushed the morgue door open and strode in with purpose. "Donny, I need to use your office phone. I can't use my cell for this."

He raised an eyebrow questioning her, but she ignored it and held up her finger. Flipping the file inside out on the missing person's page, she slapped it down on the counter and pulled the phone from the cradle. She shook her head as she dialed and waited for someone to answer.

"Hello?"

"Ma'am, is this Madeline Jardine?"

"This is Addy. May I ask who's calling, please?"

Carly took a deep breath, "Ma'am this is Detective Carly Greene of the Superior Police Department over here in Wisconsin. Could I possibly speak with your husband?" She heard the woman gasp and call for someone. Her title alone would have told the poor woman what it was about, but she was following the instructions as they were very clearly stated in the missing person's report.

The phone clanked as it was set down and picked back up, and then the voice changed. "This is Ken Jardine."

"Mr. Jardine, my name is Carly Greene, I'm one of six in the detective bureau over here in Superior. I think we've found your daughter, Juliet."

"Oh, thank god."

Carly thought it a strange response, but almost expected it from the report notes. She heard him tell his wife it was Juliet not Allison through fingers meant to muffle his speech.

"You said Superior?"

"Yes. I'm very sorry for your loss, sir."

"It's okay. It's not a shock. We knew she was dead. We've mourned and tried to begin to move on. But it'll be nice to have a body to bury, so thank you for that." There was a pause and Carly knew from many a phone call and doorbell to let things sink in and let them talk at their own pace. "Do you need someone to identify the body?"

"Technically yes. We have I.D. on her, but for legal reasons, yes. Is there someone you can send over?"

"Yes, I'll send the local police. They were involved with the case and knew her personally. Having a body to bury is one thing, but I'm not sure my wife or I could really handle seeing Juliet at this point."

"Understandable." Carly swallowed and chose her words carefully. "Will these officers be able to answer questions regarding the *circumstances* around her disappearance?"

"Certainly. So can I for that matter. Is there something in particular you want to know?"

"Well, the um, *animal* that attacked her. Do you have any photos or anything you can send of the wounds or bite marks?"

"Yes, I'm sure they've got something. They'll also know by sight. Those creatures did a number on Mackinaw, and we all saw the evidence of their attacks up close and personal."

"So what's written on this report is, um, accurate?"

"Oh yes. Yes it is, honey. Crazy as it may sound. Science gone wrong under the guise of national security and biological advancements. I'm a retired biology teacher and I had a heck of a time with these things."

"How did we not hear about this?"

"Government secrets. They covered everything up

pretty well. Paid off the victims and families, swooped in here and cleaned up the ship and creatures. They even left someone behind. They said it was for support but I don't trust that. He's still here and that doesn't make sense to me. And yet, at the end of it all, they still wouldn't admit what they had done." Another pause and Carly heard the man stutter. "I— I imagine she's pretty torn up, my Juliet."

Carly grimaced, no way did she want to tell this sweet old man what his daughter looked like now. "I don't want you to think about that, sir. Send the officers to identify and collect her. We'll let her husband know she's been found but that you are claiming her for burial."

"Okay, Detective… I'm sorry, what did you say your name was?"

"Greene, like the color with an E at the end. Carly Greene."

"Thank you, Detective Greene. I'm going to make some phone calls now. I'll send the boys over to you ASAP."

"All right. Again, I'm sorry for your loss, sir. If you need anything from us, you just call and ask for me directly."

"Okay, I will. Thank you."

The line didn't just go silent like they do with cell phones now, it made an actual audible click, and Carly smiled knowing the older couple still had a wall phone in their home.

"Animal that attacked her?" Donny was standing upright next to the body, forceps frozen in midair.

"Yeah, you're going to want to sit down for this one. They knew she was dead, they just lost the body to Lake Michigan over there at the Mackinac Bridge. A creature attack on the bridge. *Creature* being his word, not mine.

He's going to send an officer or two to identify and claim the body."

"Carly? That's the wrong direction for the current. Really the wrong direction. I mean, without tides the lakes have crazy currents to begin with, but that would mean she somehow went through the Sault Saint Marie channel. Jesus, how the—"

He glanced down at the body and Carly saw him eye the various gashes she could see. His eyes widened and his brows narrowed as he re-examined the gaping wound on her upper thigh.

"Oh Christ. I think she was snagged in a rudder right before the locks closed. She rode in on the last ship of the season, probably right to the doorstep of the Nemadji—those docks right there where you found her. She didn't have to float up from the bottom, she was probably frozen into the shoreline."

Carly curled a lip in visual disgust. "Snagged on a rudder?"

He nodded. "The torn skin is one thing, but this is the only wound that shows actual penetration into the bone. Her femur is broken, but it's also scraped all to hell. I'll do some silt and sand tests for the bay, and look into some of the wounds for evidence of barnacles or other large ship debris, and we'll see what we've got. He said he was sending someone?"

"Yes, officers who dealt with the matter."

"And they'll be able to identify the attack marks?"

Carly nodded, looking the body over. Creature might be the right word for this. If this was all done before the lake got ahold of her, whatever it was had been hell-bent on destroying her. She couldn't tear her gaze away from the large gash on the neck and Donny's voice startled her free.

"You need to get out to Allouez. *This* case is apparently open and shut and done. We have other issues to deal with." He glanced around his crowded morgue.

"I need to call Mikey about the husband, too." Her lips rose in a crooked half-smile. "Never mind. Guilty or not, he could probably use some time in the tank. I'll tell Mikey when I'm done in Allouez."

CHAPTER EIGHT

Carly almost stopped at President's Liquor, thinking a bottle of Patrón might not be a bad thing. Instead, she sighed and followed Donny's instructions, turning left at the light instead of right into the liquor store parking lot. Taking a right onto Itasca she slowed to a crawl, watching for the signs Donny said would be obvious. Two blocks later Carly saw what was clearly the beginning of the Native American neighborhood.

He wasn't kidding, was he?

Three houses in a row had banners hanging off their front doors on flagpoles. Over the years she'd seen suburban homes with seasonal banners or some overly cute imagery they either identified with or found irresistible. Here the flags were the crest of the Fond du Lac tribe, and Carly recognized it immediately from the signs at the casino across the bridge in Duluth. The colorful wheel of words with the arrowhead at the center easily marked the homes of tribe members and she paused in front of the trio, wondering which one held Granny Two Fingers.

An older teenage girl sitting on a porch with a book glanced up at her and then returned her attentions to the pages in front of her without so much as a pause for recognition, approval or otherwise. Two boys in their early teens, possibly pre-teen, were practicing skateboard tricks in the driveway of the second house and stopped to turn toward her. She could almost feel their desire to be confrontational and wondered if it was a close-knit community type protective thing, or just teen boys acting up because she was a cop. Carly may have driven a boring black unmarked Ford Interceptor, but she knew she was always recognized as law enforcement. Usually immediately.

She rolled her window down and motioned for the boys. The hesitation in their eyes wasn't fear but rather caution. The taller of the two finally walked toward her car.

"What you want, lady cop?"

Carly sighed, it was better than some things she'd been called over the years.

"I'm looking for Granny Two Fingers." Carly watched both boys expressions become that of shock. Apparently you didn't just pull up and brazenly ask for Granny.

"No way. I ain't getting tanned for that." The taller replied, as the shorter looked around the backyards he had a view of but Carly couldn't see from the street. "You go talk to Merwin. Two houses down on the left. The white one with the spear over the door."

He walked back into the safety of the back half of the driveway and Carly heard the other kid, "What you go talking to her for? Dad ain't gonna like that."

"Cos Ma would tan my hide for being rude to authority. I didn't tell her nothing, just told her to go see Uncle Merwin."

Carly slowly crept forward two houses, as the boys' conversation faded behind her. She saw the house immediately and pulled her car to the curb.

There was no banner hanging off the porch of this house. A spear, just as she'd been told, was on hooks above the door. A rainbow's worth of cloth strips and at least one feather hung off the right side of it in a clump of colors she imaged twisted to life in a breeze. The white house desperately needed a fresh coat of paint and likely looked more tan than white during the height of winter, but otherwise was well kept—the windows appeared almost too clean, the gutters maintained, the lawn perfectly manicured.

A man sat on a birch bench on the porch and watched Carly with dark eyes. She wouldn't say the expression was concern or even defensive, but rather like he was studying her for a future sketch artist and needed to catalog every detail.

"Excuse me, sir. Are you Merwin?" She climbed from the car and gently shut the door behind her.

"I am." He acknowledged with a barely perceptible nod. "What can I do for the city of Superior?"

"Is it really that obvious?" She walked up the path to the steps but stopped short at the bottom of them, holding her badge up to verify his suspicions.

"It is."

"Detective Greene." His short answers unnerved her. "We've run into a little problem with the burial site at St. Francis."

"That's not a burial site. That's a disgrace."

"Well, regardless…" She didn't disagree, but also didn't want to get into an argument or blame game or some other notion meant to put her on the defensive. She tried to maintain an air of professionalism. "The thaw has risen the Nemadji higher than normal, and washed a bit of shoreline away. There are exposed…" She paused trying to find the right word.

"Ancestors. They're ancestors. Not bodies or corpses or just things. And we don't discuss our ancestors with outsiders." His stern tone and short angry sentences made Carly think of every principal ever portrayed. Gruff and mean and always putting their foot down with every ounce of authority they had.

She swallowed, and thought maybe she could get on his good side. "But I'm not an outsider. I have native blood. Ojibwa Chippewa from the Bad River tribe over in Ashland."

"You're not Indian. You have Indian blood. There is a difference."

Carly looked at him quizzically, she'd have to follow his lead to get anywhere with him.

"You're not enough. Not everyday. You're only *Indian* when it's convenient. Otherwise, you're a white woman. And outsider."

"No. I'm a white cop, and I'm here officially. So I'm going to need your help." She planted her feet defiantly and appeared the upper dog in the fight, whether she believed she was or not didn't matter. It only mattered if he did.

"What do you need? What does the town want to take from us now?"

"Nothing like that. I understand the situation. And I'm sorry for the way it was handled *a hundred years ago*, but I need to talk to someone with authority in the tribe who can identify remains."

"We don't need them identified by you. You can just release them back to the tribe and we'll bury them with pride back on the point."

"I'll need that from Granny Two Fingers. According to what I've been told, she's the authority out here."

"She is. And she'll give you your consent. But you'll not be speaking to her personally. Do you have paperwork? Leave it with me. I'll get it taken care of and bring it back to you."

"I don't. But I'll come back with it."

"You do that."

"Bring it directly to you then?"

"Yes." He turned his head toward the end of the street and seemed to go into an immediate daze.

She realized he was openly tuning her out because he was done with their conversation. Carly got back in her car and waited until she was at the end of the block before she shook her head, "Jesus, *that* was fun and awkward." She made her way back out to East 2nd Street and headed directly to President's parking lot.

CHAPTER NINE

She answered the phone before she checked the screen, busily setting the freshly acquired bottle of Patrón on the floor behind the passenger seat, thankful the unmarked didn't have the metal grate between front and back seats.

"Greene."

"Oh, *you* didn't look at the screen." The lilt in Parker's voice was obvious.

"Hey. I'm a bit busy with all the dead floating around, you know? What's up?"

"Well, the dead floating around for starters. I'm heading over to the morgue to talk to Donny. Just wondering if there was anything new you wanted to share with the press or if you wanted to give me one of your blanket threats about printing this or that before I hand these in."

"Already? Really?"

"Should have done it yesterday, but things got a little sideways. I'm still ahead of the rest of them, but I won't be for long. All that's been printed is that the river has eroded and caused issues. No specifics. No mention of the Indian burial site."

"Yeah, I need to know what you're including. Can you read it to me? I'll give you an official statement if I approve."

"Official even? Wow. You're either overworked and not paying attention to your own words, or in a really good mood."

"Overworked. Lots on my mind."

"I can't read it to you, I'm driving. But if you really want me to, I can when I get to the morgue."

"Oh, yeah, that's right. You said you're going there. I'm headed there, too. I need to call Donny for some paperwork and head back out to Allouez. You can ride with me and we'll go over it."

"Ride with you? And a statement?" She heard the teasing tone change to concern. "Seriously, are you okay, Lil' Champ?"

"Meet you there." She hit the red button to end the call. Not because she needed to dial Donny. Not because her mind was elsewhere. But because he'd used *that* nickname.

When the television show iCarly became popular almost ten years ago, Carly had been in college, and well beyond the days of cute Disney shows and cheesy teenager Nickelodeon comedies. Before they'd ever dated, Parker had referenced the show and Carly almost walked out on their friendship then and there. Instead, she politely pointed out her name had no lowercase 'i' in front of it, and was actually Gaelic for *little champion*. He immediately latched onto the information and a nickname was born. Over the years, however, the moniker had come to only be used when she was feeling down, upset over something, or fried from work. His way of reminding her, with a gentle ribbing, she'd get through whatever it was.

She didn't need his cheerleading efforts right now.

Several deep breaths later she was dialing Donny to fill him in on the Native situation, and request he print the proper paperwork for her to pick up and bring back to the local tribe members for signatures. In turn he seemed thrilled, because their release meant he didn't have to waste manpower guarding the bones.

Carly glanced left as she neared the bridge over the Nemadji. She couldn't see the graveyard from here because of the bend in the river, and for whatever reason turned her head to the right instead. A red pickup truck sat on the trail meant for bikes and hikers.

She sighed and grabbed her phone to call it in for someone to go ticket the owner, but another glance caused her to squint and slow down. There was a truck and what looked like a small motorboat, but she didn't see anyone. By the time she called it in and someone got out here…

"Damn it."

She hit her blinker and pulled into the Kwik Trip parking lot to turn around. Looking over the area again as she drove past, she shook her head and grabbed her phone.

"When it rains, it pours." She dialed Officer Gunderson.

"Yes Ma'am." He had obviously put her in his phone at this point and tagged her number. *No more surprising him.*

"I just passed something fishy near the mouth of the Nemadji."

"Fishy?"

"Ha-ha. Yeah. Looks like an abandoned truck and boat. But it's out on the Osaugie Trail in that little inlet cove by the elevators."

"Okay, location and situation, *this* week? Yes, I'll agree with fishy."

"You want to head out there and meet me? Just in case it's something more than a ticket for being stupid."

"Sure. I've got Mr. Germain sitting comfortably in an interview room waiting. I'm free."

"Oh shit, the husband." A chuckle escaped. "Yeah, we don't need to question or even hold him. She was already a known corpse, they just lost her."

"Lost her?"

"Yeah, I'll fill you in later. Tell him we found his wife and she's being released to his father-in-law, and let him go. Remember to be all sugary and thank him for his time."

"Will do. Then I'll head out toward you."

She left the small residential road and followed the path through the grass to the visible trail. Carly could see the double ruts from the pickup and boat trailer. The small bump when she moved from grass to gravel was almost unnoticeable and she pulled up behind the truck a hundred yards up the trail.

"Okay, I'm pulling in there now. Take care of the husband and call me back when you're done. I'll know in just a few—"

The boat wasn't just abandoned. The faded blue hull was visible above the water line in the shallows. The boat leaned away from Carly, toward the bay. She could see the deep crack going down the side. And she could just make out red flannel floating in the silt and weeds near it. Squinting and concentrating on what she was looking at, she realized it was a person laying facedown. Or what was left of one.

"Shit," She half whispered to herself, somehow creating three syllables out of one. "Mikey, yeah, this is a problem. Don't come alone. And bring waders for everyone."

• • • • •

"Hey Carly."

The sound of Ben Sparkman's voice caused Carly to smile despite the scene in front of her, and she turned to face him.

Ben should have been the captain back when he rode along with Carly on her first year of beat detail, but he said the street was where he wanted to be and never went up in the rank as high as he should have or could have. Where Carly had gone to college for criminal justice and then went through the academy to fast track her way to detective, Ben had never wanted to be anything other than a cop—not a detective, not a chief, hell, he'd argued over the sergeant title but his wife appreciated the pay. He put his foot down when they wanted to make him a lieutenant, so they gave him the pay hike without the title. Now he rode with rookies for either their first or second year, and was in charge of the day shift of beat cops. He was like a father to most of the younger cops and a brother to those old enough to use his first name. Having him help out on this was awesome for Carly, it opened up personnel at her fingertips if she needed them—just as the chief had promised.

"Hey yourself. Glad to see you're back."

"Just in time for excitement and insanity it seems." He held out a pair of waders for her.

"True." She looked behind Ben to Mikey, "Just you two?"

"For now, we'll see what you need."

She kicked off her black flats—Carly's preferred dress shoe, for both comfort and courtesy. At five-nine she was simply a little tall for a girl. With heels on, she suddenly appeared to tower over people and noticed they immediately got defensive in her shadow. Black slacks or dark denim, a button-up shirt of sorts she could easily toss a sweater, blazer or other cover over, and her standard black flats was the uniform she'd approved with the chief years ago and had never changed. She always thought she looked like an office professional on casual Friday, but somehow people always knew she was a cop.

"You been out there yet?" Ben pointed toward the boat twenty feet away.

"No, was waiting for these. I can see their trail through the weeds, so I'm sure we can walk out without problems. Just be careful." Pulling the waders on she gave them unspoken permission to go ahead of her.

Ben and Mikey stepped into the weeds, following the shiny, broken twigs and grass left by whoever had gone out before them. Carly followed them as soon as she had the straps over her shoulders.

"Well, you don't see that every day." She caught up to Ben as he turned the flannel over, exposing the crushed face of what she presumed was the owner of the boat, Rob Ullman.

Carly had called in the plate on the truck while waiting for Mikey and Ben to show up. Digging through the truck for registration to coincide with the plate and locate a name for verification had almost cost her to revisit the cold Pop Tart she'd called breakfast. The waft of stench that came out of the vehicle when she opened the door made her initially think foul play had been at hand, as the interior smelled like Donny's morgue on a bad day. A couple deep breaths with overly puffed out exaggerated cheeks and a quick assessment of the passenger's seat told Carly there had been some sort of bait mishap. The carpet and seat were both stained, the discolor looking more like sludge than blood, even after what appeared to be a desperate cleaning. She found the name in the glove box and happily closed the door.

The owner, Mr. Ullman, hadn't been called in missing and was presumably just fishing. Driver's license description was five-foot-seven inches, two hundred forty pounds, black hair and brown eyes. What lay in front of her fit that description for the most part. The chunks of flesh missing from his shoulder and what appeared to be a broken jaw and cheekbone would maybe be blamed on an accident. If he had fallen and gotten somehow tangled in the propeller she could see the wounds being logical.

His legs being stripped of all meat to the sinew covered bones, cracked themselves in a couple places, was another story. But he didn't have a coffin next to him.

"Well, this is not a floater and not from the graves." Carly sighed in audible relief.

"Nope. And judging from the number of empties in that broke boat, I'm going to guess some kind of crazy accident that would be on one of those lists of the unbelievable."

"Still going to be one more body for Donny to have to deal with this week. If for nothing else than to confirm blood alcohol and the follow-up presumption of accidental death."

Mikey cocked his head, "Not sure he was alone." He pointed to two separate flip-top lunch coolers bobbing in the weeds to the right.

"Crap. You guys see anything?"

Ben stood up tall and scanned the area. "No, but until we have proof we can't really do anything. Will have to call his family and see if they knew if he was alone. Then I suppose we'll get the boats over here and look. Not much of a current back here. A body couldn't have gone too far. And if we don't find it soon enough, the fish will clean the bones pretty quickly. It's the wrong time of year for the lake to preserve the dead, it's dinner time for bottom feeders and flesh eaters." He turned and headed back to the truck, motioning Mikey to follow him.

"Actually, Carly, we'll take care of it if you need to leave. I'll deal with the calls and Mikey can take pictures and walk a tape around the area. Maybe we'll get lucky and find everything we need and wrap it up before nightfall."

"I do. I have to get back out to Allouez for the Indian burial issue at the cemetery. Thank you, so much. Glad to have your help on this one." She peeled the waders off and tossed them across the trunk of the squad car. As she slipped her feet back into her flats, the weight promptly pushing her shoe into soft wet clay, she decided maybe she'd switch to the ankle boots until further notice.

CHAPTER TEN

Parker met Carly at the curb outside the municipal building, paperwork and laptop in hand. He opened the door and hopped into the car before she'd come to a complete stop.

"Two birds, one stone. Figured I'd help speed up the process and just bring this to you." He waved a folder in front of her, which she assumed held the documents inside to release the bodies. "Donny said to remind you to tell them, he still has to examine any bodies found downstream to verify they were not in a coffin, because some of the coffins broke. So once he knows which are definitely tribal, he'll release them for pick-up. Oh and he asked if they were interested in cremation on the city's dime, apparently the mayor is feeling a bit guilty for history he wasn't even alive for."

"Or just trying to smooth things out before they get ugly."

"True. I wonder if there's a story there." Parker smiled but she only saw it peripherally and didn't acknowledge it.

"Speaking of, get your articles out."

"Plural?"

"Don't play coy, I know there's at least two versions. I have to approve both before you go presenting to Saul and getting my ass in trouble."

"But it's a cute ass."

"Shut up." She didn't bother looking at him, she knew the smirk on his face and she wasn't going to fall for it. She watched the road and tried to hug her anger tight. Weakness led to emotions, and she needed to focus right now.

He read while she drove. Quickly going through both

versions.

She preferred the spin on social commentary piece, but she always did. The other was the clinical hard news story— it could have been on her desk as a report. It was full of bloody details and gory truths, and she hated the idea of the public having to deal with what she dealt with on a regular basis, even if it was only imaginary and as long as it took them to read the accounts and fill in the visuals themselves. At least the other story made it an accident, a horrible one, but still an accident. And it brought up an important truth—no one involved with either the church or tribe today had *anything* to do with the events from 1915-1918.

"I need you to change *unknown coffins*, we know what part they're from and we'll match them to the gravestones and put them back. It'll just be a process that's all. And feel free to add that nets have been placed on the hillside and down river to prevent further problems with erosion until a more permanent solution can be put into place."

"Donny's really going to be able to identify those skeletons?"

"The ones in the coffins, sure. We lucked out there. That last row of stones that was washed free included a variety of ages and genders. Once he identifies the sex and approximate age of each coffin's contents, we'll be able to put them back. Unfortunately, once disturbed you do have to contact family in case they have issue with the resolution. Like if they want them moved all together to another cemetery, or cremated. And apparently, we're paying for the latter."

"And an official statement as promised?" Parker's fingers were poised over the keys on his laptop, the screen a blank page so he could wrap around her quote with whatever he needed for whichever article it went into.

"We're here. Let me think about it and get back to you on that. But they're both approved with that one little change." She pulled the car to a stop in front of Merwin's house. "I'll be right back."

She knew without looking, his facial expression was either annoyed she hadn't given him a statement or angry that she'd put it off. Or perhaps, he had realized she had intended to stall from the start. She nodded to the man on the porch as she approached. She noted the black of his hair was so stark it almost looked blue in the sunlight. His ruddy skin was the color of too many days fishing on the shoreline without sunscreen, and Carly paused for a moment with that thought. Most people she knew with naturally darker complexions didn't bother with sunscreen, she wondered and quickly concluded Native Americans were probably of the same mindset—after all, why bother?

"Good afternoon, sir. I have those papers for you." She climbed the steps and stopped in front of him. Opening the folder she pointed at the yellow plastic flags poking out of the right side of the pages. "If you'll just have Granny Two Fingers sign or initial where indicated…"

"Just put it in the basket there. I'll give it to her and have her sign it. You can come back for it tomorrow if you'd like." He pointed to a short square wicker basket at the end of the bench.

Carly thought about arguing about due process and the need for efficiency, but held her tongue.

"That will be fine. Early afternoon okay?"

He nodded while squinting in the direction of her unmarked sedan, and Carly wondered if he was trying to see Parker and if it would be some problem she hadn't anticipated. She tried to keep his attention on her and stepped to the side, blocking the car.

"Also, the medical examiner wanted me to tell you he will still be examining any bodies that are found down river, because of the problem at the graveyard there are both Indian and Catholic bodies, with and without coffins washed out in the erosion. He'll have to identify each one. Once he's determined it was a tribe member he'll release them to you."

"Understandable." He looked at her for a moment and Carly could see he was working through something internally. "What other section washed out?"

Carly debated being a bitch and withholding the information, giving him a taste of his own tight-lipped medicine. She chose to take the high rode.

"Near the founder's stone. The row closest to the edge of the hill there was partially eroded. Not all, but several. And because some of the coffins broke apart in the current and, well, to put it bluntly, against the shores and such, some bodies that were in coffins were found without."

"The founders' area?" He sat up and seemed to make an expression of concern that deepened the already heavy wrinkles around his eyes, but offered no explanation for his reaction. "I'll have the papers signed for you by tomorrow. Thank you."

She nodded and returned to the car. Carly sat holding the wheel for a moment, ignoring Parker's comment about that not taking long and considered Merwin's reaction. Were there Indians outside the tribal area? She'd have to check with the grounds keeper's records and see what she could find.

"Hey, Carly. Everything okay?" Parker leaned toward her with raised eyebrows and she blinked out of her thoughts.

"Yeah. Just seems to be more questions to this than answers."

"Sorry about that. I mean for you it sucks. For me it's just job security." He shrugged. "So what's the story with this guy." He indicated the house as she pulled away from the curb. She glanced over her shoulder and watched Merwin shut the screen door behind him as he disappeared inside, presumably to bring the papers to Granny Two Fingers.

"Oh you wouldn't— Actually…" She looked at him and narrowed her eyes. "You're from here, right? You could have told me about—"

"Whoa, stop right there. Remember, I only lived here until I was ten. Then we moved to Grand View, Michigan. I came back after college. So before you go getting mad at me, I might not actually have been old enough to learn whatever it is you think I should have known."

"Okay. Noted." She paused and smiled, taking a different approach. "Did you know the history of the Indians in that mass grave? That they were originally out on Wisconsin Point and got moved?"

"Yeah, a whole village was moved. But they're getting the land back out there now and they're putting up a museum or something."

"A Living History Center, yes. I read about it last night."

"Yeah. But that's all I know. I'm not even sure what tribe they were from."

"Okay, you're off the hook then." She turned onto East 2nd sharper than she needed and jostled Parker in his seat. "So *that* was Merwin, a descendant of the village on the point. Which, by the way, are from the Fond du Lac tribe."

"Like the casino in Duluth?"

"Exactly." She saw the look of confusion on his face. "The Indians didn't have the same borders the states did, remember. They spread out differently. The Fond du Lac are mostly in Minnesota now, but yes, this was part of that tribe."

"And this guy is a local chief or something?"

"No. Not exactly. Seems he's the *mouth piece* for the local... I don't know what she is. Elder, I guess. Maybe a medicine woman? I didn't think women were generally higher up in the northern tribes. I don't know. I just know she's the one with the power to clear those bodies out of Donny's fridge and this guy is the go-between, so I deal with him."

Carly noted the yellow police tape was all that remained of the abandoned truck and broken boat. *That was fast*, she thought and wondered if they'd just bagged boat and body and moved them to the impound and morgue respectfully.

"He seemed pleasant as *hell*." Parker looked past her. As she glanced his way to agree, she saw his expression darken. "What's going on at the graveyard today?"

"Nothing. Why?" She turned to look out her window. From the top of the small hill before the Nemadji bridge she could see several flashing yellow lights in the general area of the cemetery. "Oh Christ. This just keeps getting better, doesn't it?"

• • • • •

"What do you mean it's a sinkhole?" Carly tried to get a straight answer out of the guy with the hard hat and clipboard, as he pretended to be in charge and barked orders at another man in a backhoe. The equipment, with the flashing yellow light she had seen from the road, was at the bottom of the dirt path that led beyond the graveyard to a small parking area by the river meant for overflow when funerals had too many cars. He was pushing earth to the left, into the darkness Carly could barely see from her vantage point.

"Ma'am, it's just a chasm. They exist. If it were under the street they'd call it a sinkhole. No biggie."

"*Detective*, not Ma'am. And I'm aware they exist, but why is this one here? Are there graves near it? You can't just go filling in holes around here while we've got an open investigation and police tape all over hell. Who told you to do this?"

"Call came from him." The foreman nodded back to the tall angular man standing next to an SUV by the caretaker's building.

"Well shut it down until I say." She flashed her badge at him as a reminder of her authority and turned to the man responsible. Carly wasn't sure if he was the caretaker for the cemetery or someone from the church. She had no way of knowing what she was up against as she strode toward him, so she put on her professional attitude and fake smile.

"Detective Greene, and you are?"

"Bryan Grimes." The man chewed on the butt of an extinguished cigar. Carly smelled no hint of cigar and wondered the last time it had actually been lit. She raised her eyebrows to gesture she needed more information than his name. He ignored her, his face becoming concerned as he watched the backhoe shut down.

"Sir? I need to know your authority here, this is a crime scene."

"No, it's not." He spat the words in a contumacious snort of opposition. "No crimes were committed here. The cops are just trying to be in control and deal with it before the Department of Health shows up with the EPA in tow. And you're not *wrong* for thinking that way, but you're *doing* it wrong."

"We're doing it wrong?" She cocked her head at his attitude and words.

"Yeah, you are." He pulled the cigar from his mouth and spit a loose piece of tobacco to the side. "You get the loose bodies out of here. Deal with identifying them elsewhere, and then bring them back and we'll re-inter them in the proper places. Meanwhile, I'm going to take care of the issues that are strictly cemetery related and have nothing to do with your unclaimed remains. For starters, filling in that sinkhole." He flicked his hand at the hard hat behind her and she heard the backhoe roar to life. "And I've got another crew coming in later to replace your nets and ropes down there with snow fencing and sod—though I give points to whoever came up with that on the fly." He held his hands out, palms up, as if presenting her the cemetery. "In a week, it'll look like nothing happened."

Carly opened her mouth to argue but couldn't. His plan was solid, his logic on target, and damned if he wasn't absolutely correct about it not *truly* being police business, they just had more resources and better restrictive authority than a church claiming private property to keep the snoops and journalists out.

"A week?"

"Well, a week after the water recedes. We'll put the fences in now and put the sod on the hillside to cover it once the river calms down. If we do it now, it'll just wash away."

"Fine." She looked the man over again. Jeans with beat up, battered, clay covered cowboy boots poking out the bottom and a lightweight tan jacket covering a black dress shirt. "And again, *who* are you?"

"I told you, Bryan Grimes."

She glared at him and wondered if he knew just how

close to getting punched he was, then she remembered Parker was in the car probably filming everything on his iPhone. She glanced over and saw him, watching everything with a discerning eye, but no notebook or camera visible.

"I'm the caretaker. Okay? I'm between jobs and it's not much, but it's something. I also volunteer at Station 3. But my *brother* works at the EPA in Duluth and he's keeping everyone away from this to save *my* job, so long as I get it taken care of quickly enough. So you do *your* job and wrap this up. I'll do *mine* and deal with the land here."

"Station 3, eh?" His reference of the firehouse in her neighborhood softened her tone. "Thanks for your service. And thanks for keeping your brother and company out of here."

"I don't know how long it'll last. I'm sure your chief has been talking to them. And how the Department of Health hasn't come swooping in here with their bulky suits and thin mindsets—"

"Guilt."

He narrowed his eyes, questioning her.

"I think most of the agencies are avoiding this because no one wants to be associated with the body dump on the hill."

"Those departments didn't even exist yet, did they?"

"Honestly, I'm not sure. But I bet the papers would spin them right out of some funding they'd rather keep." She pulled a card out of her pocket and nodded her head toward the crew behind her. "I'm going to go talk to them and then I'll get out of your hair. Call me if you need anything. Or learn anything I should know."

He didn't respond and tucked her card into his back pocket before resuming leaning against the SUV.

Carly held a finger up to Parker, letting him know she'd just be another minute or so and walked back over toward the hard hat and backhoe.

"We good, Lady?" He looked at her with all the disdain of a man who had zero respect for women in any position of authority.

"*Detective*. And yeah. But tell me what you're doing so I can answer any questions that come along."

"Like I said, *sinkhole*. Middle of the street would suck. Or a museum—did you see that in the news last year? But this is just in the middle of nowhere, at the end of the river there." He pointed with his clipboard and she saw the black hollow at the edge of the bend. "Probably been here since forever, from the amount of gases though, it's been closed off to nothing but burrowing animals and insects."

"Gases? Is that what the smell is?" Carly realized this was probably what they'd been smelling at the graveyard and down river where they found the other bodies. It explained how bones could stink.

"Nah, that's the smell of small animals rotting in the open air down there. The gases escaped and dissipated almost immediately when the bank gave way and exposed the chasm. But from the carnage inside, it looks like a lot of small critters have somehow gotten trapped in there in the last few days."

"So why fill it in?" Carly looked at the location. It was to the side of the founders' section and didn't appear to be directly below any graves.

"If the bank has a weak spot, it'll causing cave-ins *inside* on either end and eventually spread toward those graves. Then you're looking at a repeat of all this. So we're filling it in and then surrounding it with snow fencing to keep it there."

"All righty, then. Fill it in."

"Tryin' to, Lady." He turned away from her and didn't see the anger flush through her face.

She shook her head and walked away thinking, *Detective.*

CHAPTER ELEVEN

When Carly returned to the precinct parking lot to drop off Parker, she walked into the department to throw him off, but went straight through and headed to the morgue. She found it quieter in the basement, easier to concentrate on everything and make some sort of plan. She smiled at Donny as she pushed the door open.

"How's progress in here?"

"Hey Carly." She turned and nodded to the newest deputy examiner, trying to remember her name and offering a smile instead. The young girl had been there almost a year and yet Carly had the hardest time with her name.

"We're doing okay." Donny stood up. "I've got three of the coffined bodies identified one hundred percent, based on sex, age, clothing, dental and jewelry."

"Excellent." She gave him a thumbs-up. "I'm just gonna hide in the quiet of your corner desk over there if it's okay."

"Go ahead."

"And the rest?' She gave another weak smile as a thank you and walked to the L-shaped laminated desk. If it had been upstairs, it would have probably been some beautifully streaked wood from some foreign tree she'd never heard of, to go with the amazing décor in the courthouse, but down here everything was more sterile and needed easily washable, bleachable, surfaces.

"I haven't started on the other two coffins. They're both females between twenty and thirty and will be a bit harder to pinpoint, so I'm going to go back to the first two from Tuesday."

"And the random dead?"

Donny chuckled, but the deputy chimed in, "I finished

Delcourt yesterday. Now I'm on your boat accident."

Carly nodded to the girl and settled into the chair, dropping her folder on the desk in front of her. Elbows on the desktop, her head went immediately into her hands for a moment to gather her thoughts.

She sat up, flipped open the cover of her planner, and grabbed the pen tucked inside. *I'll have to write reports for all this later, so I may as well start a list of events now.* She knew writing the list would not just help later, but be therapeutic in controlling her spinning thoughts on the situation. She freely admitted to being over organized, but tried to pretend her list making wasn't as overboard as others would suggest. She began an outline of sorts.

On Tuesday they'd found two bodies, well, one and a half. On Wednesday, they'd found one, which turned out to be Juliet Germain and was completely separate. Then five coffins floating in the river—three past the bridge, two just before it. Investigation at the cemetery showed exposed remains from the hillside where the Indian burial site was—the first two bodies, sans coffins, were so far presumed to be from there. At least one of them was identified as Indian. Thursday she'd found one set of remains at the boat wreck, again, unattached to the situation at the cemetery.

She looked at the list in front of her. *That's a lot of dead for one week.*

She knew they were dozing in the chasm at the edge of the river and had put a net across the river to catch any more non-casketed bodies. Carly grabbed her phone to call the chief and suggest dredging from the cemetery to the mouth of the Nemadji, just in case there were more Indian corpses in there. She felt it would probably be better to find them sooner rather than later and reopen all the anger all over again. She glanced at the bullet list on the page. It was a lot, but it still wasn't as bad as it *felt* once she wrote it all out.

She began dialing upstairs when Ben walked through the door. She hung up and stood. "What's up?"

"Company." He moved to the side, two uniformed officers entered after him, Mikey coming in after them.

"Mackinaw?"

The taller of the two nodded and stepped forward, offering his hand. "Officer Geegan, Dan. This is Officer Greg Jarvis. Yes, Mackinaw City Police Department." He looked around the room. "Busy place."

"Nah, just a Thursday in the big city." Donny smiled and stood, turning to wash his hands.

"Never mind him, he's trying to keep his black humor healthy." She shook the officer's hand and turned to offer hers to the other. "Detective Carly Greene. How was the road?"

"The UP is the longest, most boring strip of land—" Jarvis started to whine but Geegan cut him off.

"Which is why we speed when no one's looking."

"Just like civilians." The deputy examiner piped in and Carly smiled, forgetting she was there and appreciating the sarcasm they couldn't even argue.

"I've got your girl in the cooler. Hang on." Donny wiped his hands and retrieved the body from the cooler.

Officer Jarvis was now the one looking around. Carly followed his eyes and realized it did look a bit insane down here. He pointed to the coffins on the lowered metal biers. "Exhumations?"

"Unfortunately, no." She paused, wondering how much to tell them. "River erosion next to a cemetery. Basically, a hot mess of identifying and reburying."

The officer curled a lip. "Fun times."

"Heard you had your own problems last winter."

"Oh yeah, definitely not fun times. How much do you know?"

"I talked to Mr. Jardine."

"Ah, so you know the science angle. Creep little scientifically created or altered or whatever they were creatures, by the government who won't say they did anything at all but will conveniently clean up the mess. I tell ya, I look at the front of the Inquirer differently now. Never know which of those stories might be cover-ups."

Carly looked from the cop to Ben and saw the aged beat cop smirk and shake his head.

Donny pushed a gurney from the cooler and stopped by Officer Jarvis. "Care to check these wounds against your critter?"

"Oh no, not on this one. I can't." Jarvis backed up a step.

"You sure?" Geegan stepped forward, eyeing Jarvis and acquiescing to his desperate nod. "Okay, whatcha got?"

Donny unzipped the heavy-duty black bag that would travel with them. "Now, keep in mind she's not embalmed yet. If you need it, the nose cream is right there." He nodded to the counter next to Ben.

Officer Geegan took a deep breath and swallowed. "Let's just do this."

Donny pulled the black plastic away, exposing the remains of Juliet Germain. Jarvis made a noise and turned away. Geegan simply sighed, "Aw Jules…"

"Oh, you know—knew her?" Carly cocked a head at the cop.

"Yeah." Jarvis answered without turning toward the corpse. "We're good friends with the family. And I dated her in high school."

"Small world." Mikey looked between Carly and

Officer Jarvis.

"Positive, Geegs?"

"Yeah, no doubt at all. And yeah, don't look. No way can we let Ken and Addy see her either."

"Can I ask about the animal attack marks?" Donny interrupted the officer.

"Sure. Were you told how horrible they were? We lost several dozen citizens before we got it under control." Officer Geegan leaned over the corpse and pointed to the long smooth gash along the back of Juliet's calf, the white meat exposed and raw looking. "This is the tail here." He pointed to the deep gouges in her face and neck, "These are claw marks. Vicious little fucker. The claws were long, and wicked, kinda like a badger. Where you can see the parallel gouges, that's claw. But this? This isn't right." He pointed at the large chunk of missing meat and broken femur.

"No, that's propeller. I found evidence of zebra muscles and barnacles lodged in the bone there. I think that's how she got here from there—most likely hit the propeller for damage but then snagged on the rudder or a lazy anchor no one lifted from the water."

Officer Geegan grimaced and pulled back a bit. Carly saw him glance at the other officer to check on him. He looked back to Donny and returned his attention to the body, "Teeth here," he pointed near the neck wounds he'd previously called claw marks. "So you've got teeth, claw, and a tail strike. Yeah, sorry Jarvis, she didn't jump to safety. The little bastards got her, too." His eyes narrowed on some small round wounds near the exposed soft tissue of the abdomen and jagged tears near the center of them. "This some kind of fish? 'Cos that's not our critter."

Donny looked at what the officer referred to and glanced at Carly before making eye contact with the officer, "No. Not any fish I'm aware of. You mind if I run some tests on those wounds?"

"Not at all. Long car ride, I could use food. Jarvis?"

"I'll watch you eat. I'm not so sure I could handle food after hearing that conversation."

"Oh, yeah. Sorry."

"How about a drink instead, Officer? I got this, Donny. You know where to find us when you're done." Carly ushered the cops out of the morgue to the sound of Donny's sigh and glanced sideways at his nod of disapproval.

CHAPTER TWELVE

Derek pulled the custom Mustang behind the Kwik Trip, and followed the small single lane road down to the parking lot of the boat launch. With his hand still on the girl's knee, he turned onto the dirt path marked PRIVATE that led to the abandoned grain elevator.

"Are we supposed to be out here?" She raised an eyebrow at him but a smile slowly spread across her face.

He saw her inability to mask the excitement of danger and squeezed her thigh before he put the car in first, pulled the e-brake, and killed the engine. "I won't tell if you don't. Come on."

He got out and led the girl, Brandy, out onto the narrow ledge on the side of the tall, windowless, storage building. He sat down and slapped the cement with his hand, indicating she should follow.

"You come out here a lot?" She sat down on the cement, swinging her feet over the side where they just skimmed the water below.

"I like it out here. It's quiet, it's cheap, and it's less crowded than the point or the tower. Though usually I come out here alone."

"*Usually?*" She smiled at him and he saw her perfectly applied eyeliner—he thought they called it a cat eye—lift up as she did.

"Hey, I could have said always, but that would just be a lie. And I'd hate to start a relationship based on lies."

Brandy looked down at the water, her smile fading.

"But it's not like I'm out here with a different girl every day. Promise. I really am *usually* by myself. It's just peaceful."

Sitting in the shadow of the grain elevator, night appeared closer than it actually was. The sun was sinking behind trees and buildings but not quite to the horizon yet, and the landscape behind them caused long shadows to stretch across the water. They sat quietly for a few moments. He wondered if she was debating running back to the safety of the car or if he'd saved the evening.

He'd met Brandy at the strip club down on Tower Avenue. He couldn't remember the name of it—it was never important enough for him to tell the guys when invites and suggestions were tossed around, just "Hey, let's go to the strip club." There were two clubs, right across the street from each other, which changed owners and names often, thus he never remembered what the neon sign of the moment said. No matter the owner though, the prettier girls were in the topless only club where they just walked around and served drinks literally half-naked. The other had more dancers on the *stage* but they were less attractive according to Derek. Brandy hadn't been topless *or* on stage, she'd been behind the bar. He immediately wanted to refer to her as a stripper, but she made it clear that's not what she was, and he was instantly intrigued. A couple visits to hang at the bar and talk to Brandy rather than gawking at the half-naked girls, turned into meeting for drinks somewhere other than where she worked, and a drive out to the abandoned grain elevator.

He slid his arm across her back in the lamest of movie date moves and pulled her closer.

"It *is* quiet out here— Ah!" She punctuated the statement with an abrupt scream and small jump.

"Sorry!" Derek didn't know if he'd crossed a line.

"No, not you. There." She pointed to the right, at the weeds between them and the car.

"What?" He squinted and followed her finger.

"I think it was a snake." The worry in her eyes was genuine and Derek knew if he didn't act the hero the evening was doomed.

"Doubtful, but even if it was, we don't have any snakes here that'll hurt you." Even as he said it he wondered if it was true. "Would you feel better if I checked?"

She nodded, not taking her eyes off the weeds.

Derek stood and stepped over her, seeing she'd pulled her feet up away from the water. He walked back toward the car and parking area, but hopped down onto the sandy shoreline. Looking around he found a large stick and started moving the weeds around to see if he could disturb if not scare off the snake, and again wondered if this was the dumbest thing he'd ever done. He was about to give up when he saw movement to his right, further into the weed than the stick would reach.

He was about to declare victory on spooking the snake when two very human looking eyes blinked at him. He cocked his head, "Hello?"

The girl blinked again, the sun hitting her just right and making her eyes shine like they were silver. He made out the black hair outlining her head before she seemed to vanish. He didn't know if she lay back to hide from him or went under the water. She was too far to see clearly through the weeds and way too far for him to care enough to go wading in hip deep silt and sludge.

"Not a snake. A girl." He sat back down next to Brandy. "I don't know if we interrupted her skinny dipping or if she's purposely spying on people. I say if she wants a show, we should give her one."

Derek leaned in and found Brandy's lips welcoming and soft. His hand went to the nape of her neck, and he threaded his fingers through the hair there as he pulled her closer. He felt her nails push into his back with passion as his other hand explored her chest in alternating caresses and light squeezes. When he felt her hand on his thigh, he braved the same, but rather than setting it on her thigh as he had in the car, he found the edge of her knee-length denim skirt. She moaned lightly at the insinuation of his hand and arched slightly, pushing herself against him. He followed her smooth thigh to the edge of her underpants and ran his fingertips across the front of them, hinting at pressure. As he spread his fingers to rake them back toward him, he came in contact with a familiar bulge and pulled his hand free while backing up suddenly.

"Brandy…" He squinted and looked at her skirt as if he had X-ray vision. "Do you have a dick?"

"Sorry." She grimaced, her perfect teeth surrounded by lipstick he'd willingly smeared all over. "Oh my god, I'm sorry. I thought you knew. You seemed like you…"

"Sorry?" He sighed and watched her eyes begin to shimmer, something that looked like fear crawling into the expression there. "Hey, what's wrong? I'm the one surprised here."

"You're not going to hurt me?"

"Hurt you?" Derek shook his head in disbelief. "Oh my god, hon. No. Hell no. I'm not an asshole." He grabbed her and gave her a hug. "I'm just, well, maybe you should have led with that. I mean, you're awesome and funny and smart…"

"Thanks."

"Hell, hon, you be *you*. That's great and you'll find someone. I know you will. I'm just… well, I'm not into that." He pulled away from her and smiled "It's okay. I had fun otherwise. Come on, I'll bring you home."

He stood and put a hand out to help her up, expecting to see her relax. Instead he watched her eyes widen, not in relief but with a new, different, much more worrisome kind of fear. She pulled her hand close to her face and barely moved a finger to point behind him.

Derek turned to see the black hair and silver eyes, as two snake-like black tentacles shot out toward him, slapping either side of his head. He would have thought they were cupping his cheeks in an almost motherly way until the searing white light of pain shot through his skull. He wasn't sure if they were squeezing his head or cutting into it. He watched as another tentacle shot past him and then retracted with Brandy curled tightly in its grip. Brandy's screams became muffled as he noticed he was being pulled off the cement ledge and down into the water.

CHAPTER THIRTEEN

"Therapy or recreation?" Officer Jarvis pointed to the shot of tequila Carly had retrieved for herself when she'd brought their empty plates up to the bar.

"Yes." She smiled and put it down, Jen right behind her with three beers. "Didn't know what you guys would want."

Jarvis looked knowingly at Geegan. "Just soda, we still have to drive back."

She shrugged and pointed to the empty glasses on the table, holding up two fingers for Jen to indicate refills.

"Burgers were okay?" She tried to make small talk, suddenly feeling awkward for having a drink in front of them. If only they knew what was in her car, just waiting for her to get home.

"Really good." Geegan wiped at invisible food with his fingers. "Strange that burgers in a bar are usually so much better than those at an actual burger joint."

"Well, unlike the fast food places, they use actual cow here I think." She smiled, perhaps overly playful as she saw Parker enter the doorway. When Geegan laughed she joined him a little too loudly, hoping Parker would notice.

"Hey." Parker stopped at the table, nodding to Jarvis and purposely not making even eye contact with Geegan. "Donny's done. They can take their body and go."

"Oh?" Carly noted the curt tone and wondered if seeing her with other men bothered him. *I hope it hurts.*

By his response, he took her reaction to mean he'd been harassing Donny. "I was asking questions, in person, not even near the scanner."

Geegan squinted in the dim light, "Parker? Parker Manning? Holy shit, is that really you?" Geegan elbowed

Jarvis and the second officer gave Parker a once over. "Shouldn't you be in New York with your Pulitzer and New York Times best sellers by now?"

Parker saw Jarvis look him over, but was busy glaring at Geegan. "Yes, yes it is." He turned back to Carly, "Donny wants to see you down there ASAP." He turned and left without another word.

"Parker Manning. I would never have imagined running into him here." Geegan was silently chuckling like he had a private joke he wasn't sharing.

Carly looked at Jarvis questioningly. He answered her with a question. "How's he attached to this?"

"Local reporter." Carly felt her expression changing and didn't want to go into further detail or admit he was anything other than *just a reporter*. "We should get down to the morgue." She stood and walked over to the counter, handing Jen her card to pay for the bill.

• • • • •

"Are you sure you boys don't want to stay the night and leave in the morning? Donny can keep her in the fridge another day and I'm sure the city would put you up somewhere." Carly signed the transfer papers and tucked them into the clear pocket on the outside of the heavy-duty transport bag.

"Nah," Officer Jarvis swung the keys around his finger. "I'd rather just get home and hand her over to the funeral home. We need to get this done… for the Jardines."

Carly heard the crack in his voice and realized even though he'd said they dated long ago, it was still painful to deal with the body of someone you were once intimate with. She didn't push it any further and wished them safe travels, as she shook their hands and held the door.

"Carly, I don't like this." She turned to Donny,

worried about the tone in his voice.

"What? What do you mean?"

"I just… I can't quite pinpoint what the hell is going on here." His brows pulled together and caused his forehead to wrinkle.

"The graveyard bodies or—"

"No. The other bodies. Those marks on her. They were animal. Absolutely. And they were fresh. They were not part of the attack that killed her, and they were not from any fish I know of around these waters."

"She was up on shore."

"No, remember, she was out in the water and Mikey pulled her to shore."

"Well, could she have been close enough to shore at some point to be chewed on by land animals?"

"Maybe. I guess. But those marks aren't really jumping out at me as any known land animals either. I swabbed them and am doing cultures. I'll go over them in the morning. And I think that boating accident boy, too."

"Really?"

"Yeah, I'll just re-examine to make sure. I mean, if there's something that's not indigenous roaming around here, like those damn super snakes in Florida or something. We need to know. The public needs to know. And a plan needs to be put in place."

"Jesus," Carly shuddered at the thought of the python problem they were having in the everglades. "Okay. You do what you need. I can hold the bodies as long as we need for tests."

"Check with me in the morning. The cultures should be done by then and I may know something."

CHAPTER FOURTEEN

Carly rubbed her eyes against the bright sun and pulled the locked door closed behind her. She was stunned she was so beat. She'd only had a small glass of Patrón the night before, and promptly passing out from mental exhaustion—waking on the sofa when her alarm went off on her phone. She was stiff and far from rested, but she wanted to get to Donny and back out to Allouez and see if she couldn't get things wrapped up before the weekend. Fishing season was open and the weekend would mean the Nemadji would have more traffic—or more appropriately, nosy fishermen asking questions about nets and police tape and why they weren't being told more about what was going on.

Oh, Parker's article. Remembering he would have turned in his articles the day before, she decided to stop and grab a Telegram on the way to the station.

And as if she had spoken him into existence, she looked up as she approached her car by the curb and found Parker leaning against it.

"Good morning, Beautiful. Wanna go check out a stolen car?"

She ignored his compliment, "Why?"

"Because it was found by the old grain elevator."

"And?" Feeling like she obviously needed more coffee because she wasn't catching on to whatever Parker was insinuating.

"It's a souped up 'Stang, with dual pipes and a custom paint job."

"*That* was abandoned?" She blinked as the location dawned on her. "Wait, by the old docks behind Kwik Trip?"

"Wanna bet me there's a body nearby?" He grinned

inappropriately at the dare.

She debated calling the boys, or Donny, but figured it was just as easy to check it out herself first. "I'm not taking that bet." She pulled open the door and slid into the driver's seat."

"Shotgun!" Parker ran around the other side and jumped into the car.

Carly glared at him as he ran around the car, partly because it was childish and partly because she wasn't awake enough for his act. "Really?"

"Oh come on. You smiled a little bit."

She ignored the comment, realizing she had been trying to ignore a lot of things about Parker lately. They were going to have to stop ignoring it eventually and deal with it. Just not today.

"Hang on, I haven't had enough coffee and you're talking in circles. Stolen or abandoned?"

"I don't know. Both calls went over the—" He looked at her. "Okay yes, I was listening to the scanner."

"Today, It's okay. Did anyone say anything about the location compared to the fishing accident or graveyard issues?"

"Not that I heard before I hopped in the car and came over here. I was up really early and didn't want to call or text and wake you, so I just grabbed a coffee and came to wait."

"Thank you. For not waking me, but also for the heads up."

"No problem."

"So, um, what the hell was with you and the cop from Mackinaw?"

Parker slumped as he sighed overdramatically. "Hangover from high school immaturity. That's about it."

"That's nice. We got a couple minutes ride here, how about the longer version."

"Fine." He turned and looked out the window as he spoke. "Remember I said my family moved to Grand View? I didn't mean the one by Detroit, I meant the no-post-office, not even a stop light, tiny village in the northern portion of lower Michigan. It was *outside* Mackinaw, but still in the school district. I was bussed in to the city schools, there was a lot of bus in my life. There were a ton of stops and we were on that bus for over an hour before and after school. They referred to those of us at the outskirts like that as the country kids. So I had one strike against me there. I wasn't a cool city kid, pretending to be all that when the tourists came. I was more sheltered from the bullshit. And I was writing back then—"

"Yeah, you've told me that. Short stories and poems and such, right?"

"Yeah, which is fine in elementary school, but when you get to junior high and the teachers realize it and love it and point it out, the jocks just pick on you for it. All through junior high and high school I got grief for being a writer, like there was something wrong with it."

"So you *knew* those cops. Did you know Juliet, too?"

"No, not really. She was a popular girl dating a jock. I knew *of* her, but not enough to identify her. Hell, even when you said the name it didn't click because it wasn't her maiden name. I don't even know if it would have if you'd have said it. Shame about her though. What I knew of her was that she was a sweet girl."

"And after all this time they recognized you and *still* gave you crap? Wow. You must have left a hell of an impression."

"I doubt it. I'm just chalking it up to immaturity."

"Oh I don't know. Might have been shock or black

humor in the face of gruesome death. They seemed like good guys."

"I'm sure they did." The tone in his voice said he believed anything but his own words.

Carly pulled into the Kwik Trip and followed the single lane to the abandoned grain elevator and Mustang in question—hard to miss a bright orange sports car with pinstripes. Several squad cars were already in the area and she saw Mikey running the tape roll around the perimeter. She pulled in and parked. "Stay here."

"Yes Ma'am." She glanced at him, expecting a fight but seeing him pull out his notebook instead.

Carly walked up to Ben in time to hear him dismiss the initial cops on the scene.

"Due to proximity of the other cases, we'll be handling this one. Thanks for what you've done. Go ahead and call dispatch and let them know you're back on beat." Ben turned to her. "How'd you beat Donny?"

"I cheated. I have a journalist with a scanner and sense of direction in his pocket."

"Parker." Ben nodded at the car and Carly saw Parker wave. "So you weren't even called yet?"

"Nope?" She pulled her phone out to show him and saw the screen. "Shit. Take that back. Two missed calls and a text from Babybird."

"Okay good. 'Cos I told that kid to get ahold of you as soon as I heard the address. Too close to the rest for my liking."

"What do we have, kids." Donny joined the conversation.

"Over here." Ben walked them past the Mustang, waving it off like it was a generic coupe, "No evidence of anything in the car. But it seems the owner, Derek Mullaney, brought an unknown person with him out this way." He pointed to the ledge where two officers in blue jumpers from the forensics team were squatted down scraping the pavement.

"Unknown person?" Carly questioned.

"Yeah, there are two clearly separate smears of blood out there. One seems to be a spray, heavy and sudden from the looks of it. The other is more of a smear that leads off the edge. The angles and amounts just can't be the same person, even if they were doing somersaults according to those two."

"Well, if *they're* here and the victims aren't, you don't need me." Donny pointed to the forensic team as they were heading back toward them.

"The body is over here." Ben walked past the end of the cement pathway to the weeds near the small bit of sand at the edge of the inlet.

Carly turned toward the shallow marsh, unsure how she'd missed the yellow tape around the perimeter on low sticks. Stepping over the tape, the four of them stood over the body as it lay on a black unzipped body bag.

"Already moved?" Donny asked no one in particular.

Ben answered, "They took samples and pictures and did what they do and left the body for you."

"Okay." He squatted down, pulling gloves from his pocket.

Carly wondered if he carried those blue gloves like old women in church did with Kleenex, always a tissue tucked up their sleeve. She watched as he poked at the body, checking gas content for rough time of death, Carly guessed from previous outings. He pulled the collar of the T-shirt back on the body and Carly heard her own exclamation in stereo as Ben and Mikey followed suit.

"Ohhh. What's that?" Ben leaned down.

"Are those?" Carly answered with a question to

Donny.

"They are." Donny looked up at her.

"Donny was just showing me these. I think we might have a problem, guys. I'm gonna have to declare this an official crime scene just to make it easier, and then let them do their thing on the perimeter. We'll have to send a forensic team back to where Juliet's body was found, too." She sighed.

"Donny?" Ben questioned the medical examiner.

He stood and pulled his gloves off—inside out and wrapped around each other—then tucked them in his pocket. "Here's the thing. It's... well, we don't know what it is. We only know what it's not. It's not a fish. And it's not a weapon of sorts. It's organic, but hell if I know what kind of animal is doing that."

Mikey curled a lip but Ben did the speaking, "Is it doing that to them after they're dead? Do we have a crime and then an animal picking at pieces? Or is that cause of death?"

"Judging from the lacerations in his jugular, I would say it's probably cause of death. Which means it's an animal attack."

"Oh wonderful." Mikey started looking around at the weeds and small bushes, looking for something to be hiding in them.

"But if it was an animal, would it eat him?" Ben glanced at Carly.

"There's been a lot of post-mortem damage and feeding on the other bodies, but this one looks relatively untouched. I wonder if it got spooked. Interrupted?" Donny turned to the forensic crew packing up their vehicle. "You guys get anything off this body other than I.D.?"

The male technician shook his head and put the large

toolbox in the back of the open SUV. The female shouted, "I.D. and a small bag of weed. That's it."

"Weed? You think whatever attacked didn't like the smell?" Mikey's eyes lit up like he had a plan.

"Doubtful. It appears to have pulled him into the water, which would have gotten the weed wet and killed any residual aroma." Donny bent down and pulled the bag over the corpse, zipping it shut. "Wanna help me get him into the wagon?" He looked up at Ben.

"Back to the morgue?" Carly questioned, knowing she still had to run out to Allouez.

"Yup. I need to look at our fishing accident."

"Oh shit. I hadn't even thought about that one." Carly knew it wouldn't take him long. "Okay, I'll meet you down there and get the skinny on whether that one has these marks and gets moved to the growing pile of questions on my desk."

CHAPTER FIFTEEN

"An animal? Shouldn't we call in the DNR or someone?"

"Not yet. Not until cause of death is actually blamed on it. If it's just scavenging after the fact, that's normal, even if the animal isn't from these parts. It becomes a whole different thing."

"Jesus the red tape you play with… and the animal evidence has been on all the corpses?"

"Not confirmed yet. Donny's working on that."

As Carly drove straight across East 2nd rather than turning right to go downtown, Parker leaned against his door, turning toward her.

"Oh excellent, I love an adventure."

"No adventure. Just, we're this close and it's become such a habit now, I figured we'd drive past the cemetery. I want to know if they got that chasm filled in or not." Carly pulled into the cemetery.

The yellow police tape had been torn free and was lying on the ground. The caretaker's SUV was sitting next to the little building, exactly as it had been last time she was there, but she didn't see Mr. Grimes anywhere. The building's windows were dark, so she assumed he wasn't inside, and it was likely closed and locked. She drove straight ahead, planning to check with the hard hat, when she saw the backhoe was tipped over. She hit the brakes, slowing down drastically and looking around the graveyard.

"What?" She saw Parker watching her behavior. "Carly, what?!"

"There." She nodded ahead of them at the tipped equipment. "I gotta go check it out." She crept the car halfway down the hill and put it in park.

Getting out, she pulled her gun from her side, unsure if it would help but feeling better with it in hand.

"Mr. Grimes?" She called and walked toward the backhoe. As she reached the bottom of the gravel road, she scanned the parking area. Seeing nothing, she walked around the side of the backhoe.

"Mr. Grimes?" She yelled again, wishing she knew the name of the workers so she could call for them, and immediately wondering if she shouldn't keep quiet until they knew what kind of animal they were dealing with. Her right foot sunk down in the wet red clay and she pulled it out with anger and an overreacting sense of fear.

And then she saw the caretaker.

The chasm had been almost filled in when she'd left the previous afternoon. Now it stood like a gaping maw on the side of the riverbank. The caretaker's body laying half in the river next to it. His face appeared to have marks on it like the Mustang owner had, but his neck seemed to be turned at an impossible angle. His hands were black with mud *or blood*, Carly guessed they were defensive marks or trying to crawl away maybe. One cowboy boot was missing, and the coinciding pant leg was torn to shreds, exposing the truth beneath—the meat of his leg was completely missing and the gleam of bone shone in contrast to the dirty water around it.

She looked around again. There were no signs of the workers. Carly realized she had no idea if they'd been there when it happened and were now missing, or if they hadn't come to the job site yet today.

Worried about an unknown animal, she glanced over the wet clay and mud of the parking area, looking for tracks. She saw nothing but human footprints, the treads of the backhoe, and what looked like a shovel or something being dragged. She swallowed and headed back to the car, pulling her phone as she did.

"Lucas, find Ben and patch me through." She wished the old man would use a cell phone, but understood he preferred his collar mic and car radio. *Old ways for the old timers*, he would say.

She reached the car and tapped on Parker's window. He rolled it down and looked up at her without words.

"We've got at least one dead. I don't know if the workers were here or not, but the caretaker is down there. I can't leave a scene with a body until someone shows up. Can I leave you here until Ben gets here?"

"Um, hell no. Without a vehicle to hide in or a gun to borrow? Absolutely not."

She nodded, fully understanding his answer. "Okay, then we wait."

• • • • •

Ben had arrived with Mikey, two field evidence technicians, and another cop the chief had given him to help out. Carly had basically pointed in the general direction of the body and left with Parker to meet Donny at the morgue.

Parker stood quietly at the end of the metal gurney, patiently and politely keeping his mouth shut.

"So?" Carly watched as Donny moved across the body.

"Yup. Here we go. Same marks." He pointed to the open tear on the left shoulder.

"That's not propeller?"

"I completely would have said that on the paperwork, but now seeing the little circles here and here," he pointed under the arm up high on the rib cage and on the back of the shoulder, "it's got to be our unknown."

"So cause of death is animal? We give this whole thing to the DNR?"

"Not quite so fast." He shook his head and a part of her was relieved. She hated the local DNR guy, or rather *Fish and* Game, and didn't want to concede anything to him.

"First we call in animal control to see if it's something to be trapped or contained. They'll call Fish and Game for assistance if they want, but the jurisdiction is in city limits so they won't have to."

Carly nodded, following along.

"All the bodies were in that one strip of land along the Nemadji, right?"

"The Indians and coffins were erosion on the hillside. Our fishing victim here, and presumably his partner—"

"Partner?"

"Oh yeah. His wife said he went out fishing with a friend. There's no sign of the friend so far."

Donny shook his head.

"Then we have the Mustang couple. And the caretaker."

"And that's the one you just found?"

"Yeah. You gonna go look at the wounds?"

"No point rushing. They'll bring him back here once they clear the scene, I'll look when he gets here. Wanna take a guess?"

"No. He had a slash on his face and the flesh of one leg was completely gone. Looked familiar enough for me to safely guess without losing a wager. Now if the workers are down there, in the chasm maybe, 'cos I didn't go looking and messing with evidence, then that would be two more. So yeah, all along the river there."

She looked up from her fingers where she'd been ticking off bodies and saw Donny giving her a strange look.

"What chasm?"

"Oh, that development just came to light yesterday. Seems a cave-in near the edge happened. A big one. I mean—" Her focus drifted off for a second in thought before she snapped back to attention, "Donny, what kind of wildlife lives in or near caverns by the water?"

"Oh hell, hard to say. A lot. Anything from otters, beavers and such to snakes, turtles, whatever. And again, I can't quite pinpoint the animal we're looking for by the wounds. They don't match any teeth, tusks or talons in the database for the region. I'd have to get inside there."

"Well, they were trying to fill it in. Actually, they were filling it in yesterday and it was completely exposed again today." She paused, making a note to herself to ask someone later. "Though, you know, I'm not so sure I'd be comfortable with you going in there. Maybe a diver with a suit, not that they could see underwater, but at least if it caved in again, they can drop down into the river and have an oxygen tank to get them out of there."

"Well, okay. I can see the danger inherent considering the high water and existing erosion issues. Where along the cemetery is this cavern?"

"Oh it's well below the graves, I don't imagine the graves falling is a problem." She assumed that was his concern due to his comments about the current situation. "As far as location, it's just beyond the founders' corner, by those really old sunken stones in the little woods there."

"Carly." He looked at her intently, as if she should know what he was thinking. "If there's something living in caves along the river, you know who would know about them."

She shrugged, then realized what he was hinting at. "Ohh, sure. They've hunted the land and water all around that area for longer than anyone else in the region. You're right. And I need to get those papers for you anyway, so I was heading out there. I'll ask. Though that guy is not very friendly, is there something I can do or say or bring that will get him to open up?"

It was Donny's turn to shrug, "Doubtful. Good luck."

CHAPTER SIXTEEN

Merwin stood as soon as Carly pulled up to the curb. As she climbed the steps, she noticed he was *not* holding any papers and she worried there was going to be a problem.

"Follow me, please." He opened the screen door and held it for her to walk past him.

The interior of the house was somehow *nothing* like Carly expected. For whatever reason, she thought it would be colorful like their banners and decorated with walls full of history. Instead, it was mostly exposed hardwood rather than painted walls or carpets, giving it a much older feel than the 50s style house should have had—it felt almost turn of the century. Carly could smell the wood and was reminded of her grandfather's cabin. *Better than air freshener*, she thought, *the scent of nature and memories*. There was a patterned blanket thrown on the back of the couch, but otherwise the décor was very minimal with a line of portraits in a variety of mediums on the living room wall, seeming to mark generations with style and canvas material.

Merwin walked Carly straight past the living room to the long rectangular table in the dining room. Bare but for a bowl of rocks and flower blossoms, the formality of the room felt again out of place in her assumptive mind.

"Would you care for a drink? Coffee? Soda?"

"No. But thank you." She paused, wondering why the sudden change in his behavior. "Do you have that paperwork?"

"I do, but Granny Two Fingers would like a word with you."

"Oh, okay."

Perfect, Carly thought. *I'd rather ask her about the*

animal attacks than you.

Merwin disappeared and a small Indian woman appeared. She was barely five feet high, with a thin, frail looking frame, but her eyes held strength and knowledge that commanded respect immediately—the stark green of them unusual for a full-blood native.

"Oh, he knows I hate this stuffy room. Let's move to the living room, dear." She walked back the direction Carly had just come from. Carly stood and followed, finding the woman had already settled on the couch with the throw pulled off the back and over her legs. Carly chose the stuffed chair opposite her.

"I'm sorry for Merwin, dear. He thinks everything is a conspiracy and no one should be trusted. I have your papers, but I had a few questions."

"No problem, Ma'am."

"First of all, call me Granny Two Fingers, or Granny. Ma'am is just too much. And your name?"

"I'm sorry. Detective Carly Greene."

"Greene with an E at the end?"

"Yes, why?"

"Hmmm that is a Lake Superior tribal name. Are you local?"

"Oh, no, my family was from Ashland. But I do have Ojibwa blood from Bad River."

Granny nodded, "Explains the beautiful shine to that black hair."

Carly felt a blush wash across her face. "Thank you." She noted for a *Granny*, the woman had the same deep black hair she did, with only a few strands of silver to betray the beginning of her graying, though judging by her appearance, Carly would have presumed her well into the years of silver hair and wondered if she dyed it for vanity, appreciating the long thick braid that lay across the woman's shoulder.

"Your hair is equally beautiful."

Granny looked down at the braid, which fell below her breasts. "Thank you. You know," She leaned forward and spoke with a smile, as if telling an old friend something forgotten. "I wear it like this because I once told someone, *if I ever cut it, perm it, or otherwise look like a poodle in my old age, I need to step down.* And I'm not ready to step down."

A quick once-over also showed Carly the woman had deep wrinkles, but there was a smoothness to her skin that made Carly believe it probably felt like tissue paper. The woman's hands were tipped in short clipped nails that had seen a fair share of work but still somehow had a better manicure than her own. Carly's own nails were forever in a state of chipped polish—the tips of even a fresh coat always seemed worn off within hours. She blinked away from her nails and looked back to Granny Two Fingers.

"You said you had questions?"

"Yes." Granny Two Fingers pulled a small pipe from folds of her wrap. It appeared to be carved bone, or a quality imitation. She held it up to Carly, "I quit eons ago, but I still like to hold it when I'm thinking. It's a harmless crutch at this point."

She smiled and Carly noted what had to be dentures considering their perfect shape, size and spacing for her age. Carly approved, keeping her lips closed in a polite grin, rather than broad smile.

"The paperwork simply says the bodies are released to us. What if we were interested in cremation? Would the city be willing to do that for us?"

"Really?" Carly had gone online and searched, learning the traditional funeral practices were to wrap the body in birch bark and bury them shallow so they could travel. She didn't see anywhere where cremation was used or even approved of.

"Well, we cannot know who is who in there. And therefore, we cannot celebrate the individual. The mothers have long since passed as well, so there will be no need for the year of mourning or the hair dolls. But perhaps, if cremated, we could scatter them out on the land of their original interment and they will find their ways back to their proper places."

"I'm sure that wouldn't be a problem."

"Excellent. And if you could ask whether exhumation of the rest of them is possible. Now that we have that land back on the point, I'd like to return all of them."

"I will talk to those in charge and find out for you. If it would make things right after all this time, I'm sure they would be more than happy to accommodate."

"The papers are on the table by the door," She pointed behind Carly and the detective turned, spying the small side table.

"Can I ask *you* a few questions, while I'm here? Seems we've run into an issue in the river you may be able to help us with."

Granny Two Fingers nodded.

"Some of the bodies," Carly chose to leave the idea of murder or fresh death out of the conversation, "have had marks on them we're unfamiliar with. Your people have hunted and fished this land for centuries. Do you know of anything in the waters or marshes that would not normally behave like a carrion that we're not considering."

"Nothing in the marshes. The land animals are all prey rather than predator around there. An occasional coyote may come in and snag one of them. Large birds of prey? I know I've lost a fair share of kittens to the owls around here."

"I don't even know if they'd considered birds yet. I'll have to ask."

"But the water? Maybe there. When my grandfather used to spear down near the river mouth, he would come home with tales of strange eel-like fish. My brother caught one and it turned out to be nothing more than a northern pike with strange colors. If you're looking at crazy teeth marks, I would blame the pike and random musky." She shrugged. "Though, that lake is vast. And it connects to many rivers. Maybe there are things deep down that have just grown out of proportion." Something about the way she spoke, her eyes glazing over as if she were remembering the information she relayed like it had been her, not relatives.

"Okay. So maybe just look for larger versions of the more predatory fish?"

"The sturgeon and lamprey can get very large if left alone in these waters."

Carly shuddered. She hated the very idea of lampreys, like giant leeches with teeth, and saw herself avoiding the fresh water for the time being in lieu of a kiddie pool in her backyard. *Lampreys though, they have that circular bite.*

"Do you know of anything else that has a bite like the lampreys? We have some circular wounds on the bodies. Most notably on the one near the chasm. Is there anything you know of that lives in the mud on the banks that would leave marks like—"

"Chasm?" Granny Two Fingers leaned forward, putting the end of the pipe in her mouth and chewing on the bone nervously. "Where?"

"It's just a sinkhole. Near, or rather below, the founders' corner of the cemetery. Big old cavern that had gases and such in it, according to the workers trying to fill it in."

"Did they go inside?" The worry on her face was evident and Carly started to feed off the expression and become concerned herself.

"I'm not sure. It sounded like it wasn't sturdy and would eventually threaten the rest of the shoreline, so they were just concerned with filling it and then fencing the side against future erosion."

Granny Two Fingers looked out the window, her gaze distant. She spoke to Carly but seemed to address the view outside the glass. "You don't just have marks on the long dead. You have new bodies, don't you?"

Carly debated holding back information, but having not seen the paper yet, she had no idea if it was out about the accidents and didn't want to burn bridges by openly lying to the woman. "Yes. There have been a couple accidents in the area."

Granny Two Fingers turned and looked at Carly, holding her gaze captive with eyes suddenly very clear, youthful, and full of fear. "They were not accidents."

CHAPTER SEVENTEEN

Steven Booker left Allouez and drove north on East 2nd toward the FedEx Ground hub in Superior. He'd only had forty drops and half as many pickups, light for a Friday, and was heading back to park the truck for the weekend. As the owner/operator of a ten-route delivery business, subcontracted to FedEx, Steven knew that while the deliveries were done for the day, the paperwork was not. He needed to go over mileage and schedule downtime for the trucks due for preventative maintenance services. He grabbed his phone and dialed his manager, tossing the phone back into the cup holder and hitting the button on his blue tooth headgear.

"Hey Steve, what's up?" His manager picked up on the first ring.

Prompt and efficient, Steve always liked that about him. The manager usually drove the short route, and would have been driving except for the cast on his leg, which meant he was desk and Steven was driver in reversed roles for the next eight weeks.

"Hey Doug. I'm done with your route. Not much to that one is there?" He didn't wait for an answer on the rhetorical question. "I'm going to park back at the hub and head over to the office. Can you hop on the cloud and check mileages and PMs. Call Otto and get them scheduled. Then I can just deal with the weekly reports when I get back and… Oh hey, hang on."

The truck chugged black smoke and lurched, dropping speed from forty-five to barely crawling along at fifteen like he'd slammed the brakes.

"Whoa." Steve let off the gas and pulled the truck to the side of the road, coasting rather than purposely braking, as he listened to the engine and watched the dash gauges for any indication of what was going on.

"Steve?"

"I'm okay. Truck just decided it wasn't. When was the last time your truck was in?"

"It was just down last week for new injectors."

"Oh this had better not be a warranty problem. I'm so done with that guy and his faulty injectors." Steve turned the truck off and set the flashers to blink. "I'll call ya back. I gotta call Otto."

Steve didn't wait for an answer, disconnected the call and speed dialed Schantz' Shop.

"Schantz's," The gruff voice trying so hard to be friendly was unmistakable.

"Otto. It's Steve. Doug's truck just blew up out on East 2nd. Can you come look at it?"

"Dead dead and needs a tow, or just gimpy?"

"Gimpy. Maybe. It blew black smoke and slammed me forward as the speed dropped to about fifteen real sudden. Who did the injectors last week? It wasn't that punk mechanic you have, was it? His work is always coming back."

"Nah, I fired him a while back for being a lippy bitch. I'll hop in the service truck and be out in a few. Where you at?"

"Northbound lane on East 2nd. Right before the Nemadji river bridge."

"Okay. I'll be out."

Steve hit the button on his headgear to disconnect the call and slammed a fist against the steering wheel. He screamed nothing coherent just to get it out of him and leaned back. It was Friday. It should have been an easy day. He should have also known better. Easy days are few and far between.

He glanced over at the marsh that led to the strip of

water some called a bay but was really nothing more than an old channel for the boats to get to the grain elevators. Most of the elevators were no longer in use, the bigger ships preferring the deeper waters of the west gate basin near the train yards. Smaller private boats now used the old elevator bays for docking and fishing. The weeds split suddenly, like a piece of wood under an axe and he saw a flicker of movement.

Muskrat or musky, he thought. Beavers, otters and muskrats had been moving in to the area in the last few years, and while they were a nuisance to land owners and lumberyards, he'd always thought they were cool animals. On the other hand, he hadn't been fond of muskies since he'd been a boy and his uncle had landed one longer than he was tall, pulling it into the boat still thrashing while Steve curled into a fetal position to hide his fingers and toes from the nasty rows of sharp teeth.

His curiosity won over his fear, and he decided it was marshlands rather than open water, thus, not a musky. He grabbed his phone and got out of the truck, snagging the stack of collapsible hazard cones as he did. Dropping them behind the truck in a line to warn drivers, per regulation, he looked around him before stepping into the field at the side of the road.

While some guys thought it was spring enough for shorts, Steve was still sporting uniform pants and walked through the tall grass without worry of thorns or old dead burrs to catch on his legs. He neared the spot he'd seen the animal and stopped. Watching the area intensely, he listened for any noises that may give it away, holding his phone out in front of him, camera at the ready. He smiled, knowing his fiancé would love a picture of one of the little critters up close. Movement to his left caught his attention and he turned in time to see the tentacle flatten in front of him, and slap him directly in the face. He felt the suckers on the under side move across his cheek slowly, slurping like a child's tongue tasting its way along a spoon of cake batter. The small cups squeezed suddenly, gripping his flesh before tearing it away from him.

He thought he screamed, but he didn't hear it.

CHAPTER EIGHTEEN

"Our legends, like so many around the world are just stories… tales mostly. Meant to entertain adults and scare children. But not this. No." Granny Two Fingers' forehead had become a field of deep wrinkles, her expression that of grave concern, and her gaze elsewhere.

She finally turned to Carly, "Trapped by only the bravest during mid-winter's moon and sealed up in the hard clay which the sun dried to hold her tight. Several were lost in the battle. None were forgotten. As those left behind planted mighty trees above her that their roots may seek her out in the soil and further encase her. My great-grand pappy's grand pappy helped fortify her prison. She's very real."

"Who?" Carly thought they'd been talking about an animal, but now suddenly *it* was a *she.*

"Gete-Oga. The ancient mother." Granny Two Fingers leaned forward, her voice had been the harsh whisper of age and whiskey, but it sounded suddenly very clear. Commanding in a soft tone, as if telling an important secret. "You see, dear, gods do not give birth to other gods, demigods, or even heroes. Their offspring are monsters, mutants, and abominations. And *this* is the mother of them all."

"It's a monster?" Carly felt the twinges of disbelief crawling at the base of her skull like a blossoming headache.

Granny Two Fingers shook her head. "Don't think me a crazy old woman, child. Listen to me."

The fear and urgency in her voice forced Carly to hold her own doubt at bay. She would at least hear the woman out and appear to play the part, after all, many a myth was based in reality. Maybe she could work backwards to the truth if she listened to the twisted legends. She retrieved her notebook and pen from her pocket and flipped it open to a blank page. After writing GRANNY 2 FINGERS at the top, she nodded at the woman, urging her to continue.

"This is the *mother* of the monsters. The whore of the gods. She's been used and discarded by things more ancient than time. Abused by that which *we* fear in the dark. Bled and bred with, by the original nightmares, to spawn the shadows of myth." There was a strange mixture of fear and sadness in her eyes, as they glistened with tears held at bay.

"Do not confuse it with gods and monsters. It is not Wendigo, Mishebeshu, or Nibiinabe. It was made by the creator god to satiate the others. It is not their equal. It is only where they have lain, and left their seed. And it is cursed. Timeless. While you need not fear her, you should fear her visitors, and children…"

Granny Two Fingers chewed on the end of the old bone pipe and looked beyond Carly to someplace else. Carly could see the woman's mind working around something, while her own rolled through the words she'd just heard. She had so many questions. And surprisingly, believed that the woman at least believed her own words.

"Wait… What are the other things you mentioned?" Carly focused on the myths she'd never heard of before for reference.

"Wendigo—"

Carly cut her off, shaking her head and holding out her hand. "Sorry, no, I know that one. The other two."

Granny nodded, "Mishebeshu was in charge of all the other water monsters. He was a monster himself according to the lore, *not* a god. He was a powerful mythological creature—a cross between a cougar and a dragon. He was, as I said, in charge of the other water monsters, but he himself was known to cause men and women to drown. When the great lake took victims, it was said Mishebeshu had collected them."

Granny turned to the small hutch against the wall and stood. "I may have something…" She opened the lower right door and Carly could see a handful of books, something wrapped in what looked like a pelt of some sort, and several bundles of burnt sage at various levels of use. "Yes, here, this may help."

Granny pulled the thin blue book from the cabinet and shut the door. She laid the tome on the coffee table in front of Carly and opened it, revealing a mix of printed words and handwritten notes throughout the text and in the margins. Flipping through the pages she stopped and pointed to a drawing. The caption beneath it said Mishebeshu. Carly nodded and Granny flipped several more pages. A mermaid looking creature with Native features was captioned Nibiinabe.

"This was another race. Water spirits. But these are also myth. Everything in this book is myth, whether based on something real or not."

"And Gete… Gete-Oga?"

"She's not in the book. There are many things in the book. But there are a great many things which are not." Granny Two Fingers stared at Carly for a moment.

Carly thought it looked like she had much to say but didn't know the words, or perhaps wasn't allowed by tribal law. There seemed to be something desperate behind the woman's eyes.

"So myths. If they are all just myth—"

"Oh child. Who's to say what's myth and what's not until it crosses your path?"

Granny held up her left hand and Carly saw the index

and middle finger were missing. *Granny Two Fingers, I get it.*

"I saw this myth, on a cold winter night by the barely there light of a sliver moon. I thought it Wendigo and put my hand out to stop it. It took my fingers and ran at the taste of them. It was just a wolf. A wolf who knew my magic was stronger and thought better of finishing the job." She nodded to the rug on the floor under a basket of magazines, a smile in her eyes but not on her lips. "I caught up with him later."

"But Gete-Oga?"

"Not in the book. Not a myth. *Anything* but a myth."

"You said not to fear her, but she's killing—and maybe eating—people."

"Honey, you answered your own question. She's not hunting or stalking or scaring for pleasure. She's just hungry. She's been buried for over five hundred years in that mud. She's not leaving meals behind unfinished. She's being spooked away. How many missing have been reported with no signs of their misadventures? No bodies or property? Just… gone."

"What does she look like? What am I dealing with?" Carly glanced through the bizarre drawings in the book and thought of the strange markings that had been on the victims. She wondered if they were caused by teeth or claws, or nothing more than an unrealized logical answer hidden inside mythological smoke.

"That part is legend. Although, the most commonly agreed upon description was that of a human-squid hybrid. I believe they're called cecaelia in other parts of the world. Like a mermaid, but with tentacles rather than a tail. Of course, even those words—passed down from the warriors who last saw her half a millennia ago—are scrambled and don't always match."

"So I'm looking for a squid woman?" Carly felt disbelief crawling back in.

"You're looking for an intelligent creature with a history older than this country. Stories claim she is striking, though not beautiful. And much like sailors were swayed by mermaids, I imagine she found victims by hiding her lower half and luring lonely men to what they thought was a helpless female."

"And what do we do?"

"Trap her." Granny spoke with a curtness of tone that indicated it should have been the obvious answer. "Legend says she's cursed to live forever. That she cannot die. That is why she was trapped."

"But they may not have had the methods, and definitely not the weapons we have now. I mean," Carly couldn't leave with fantastical creatures and no plan, one or the other had to give, "you said she's not a god. Just an animal. *And animals die.*"

"This particular animal is older than time. At some point… death means nothing."

Granny stood back up, closing the book and returning it to the cabinet. Her fingers hesitated over the faded tan book next to it, but she pulled her hand away empty. She settled back onto the couch, pulling the blanket over her and suddenly appearing to be her previous aged, tired self.

"Your paperwork is signed and sitting there by the door. Use the knowledge I've given you." She tucked the pipe back into the folds of her wrap and nodded politely at Carly, releasing her as if she'd been summoned. "Don't make the same mistakes that have spawned nightmares of old things in the past."

CHAPTER NINETEEN

"Donny, I don't even know what to think of what that woman just told me. Could you please tell me something scientific I can wrap my head around?"

"Sure, Carly." She heard a metal clink noise and realized she was on speaker and he was still working on bodies. "Your caretaker here? Same marks."

She sighed. "Yeah, that's super helpful. Fuck. Okay I need to do some research and see if I can convince myself to believe this insanity."

"That bad?"

"Old Indian legends and myths and monsters and—oh my god, I need a drink."

"So lunch it is then?" Carly could hear the snark in Donny's tone.

"Maybe. Yeah." Not even defending her alcohol abuse as of late, because she knew full well Donny and everyone else in her life knew it was a temporary thing to deal with the bullshit of her current relationship hell, she nodded to herself at Donny's suggestion and decided to do just that. "But first, I'm going to leave you with something you never saw coming. Squid."

"Excuse me, squid?"

"Squid. Could those circular marks be from a squid?" Carly tried to make what Granny Two Fingers had said and the evidence they had in front of them match up on some level.

"Well, I… um… Okay, a couple things. First off, I don't know jack about squid, but I'm pretty sure they don't live in fresh water." She could almost *hear* his brows furrow in confusion. "Secondly, if they did, I wouldn't recognize a bite."

"So here's the thing, Donny. Humor me. Look it up.

Check the swabs against the salt-water database or squid family or whatever. But put your brain on a shelf and take a trip down Woo-Hoo Crazy Lane with me for a bit. Check those wounds against possible squid attacks."

"I don't know if you're already drinking or just trying to drive me to join you, but okay. I'll play along. It's not like I don't have a morgue full of bodies to process."

"That's just identifying, give that to the deputies. I really do need you to do this. Because if it's not, then my ability to judge people is all fucked up right now. And if it is, I have absolutely no idea how to proceed."

"All right. But I'm going to feel like a fool doing this."

· · · · ·

"You eat anything today?" Jen pushed a second shot glass of tequila across the bar at her.

Carly squinted one eye and looked at the ceiling while she thought, as if the answer would be written there. She shook her head, realizing the days had begun to blur. "A day-old donut count?"

The bartender playfully slapped her forehead, and then pushed several buttons on the small computer screen near the register.

"You know Parker was in." It was less a question and more an informative statement of guilt. "He doesn't even drink when he comes in here anymore. It's weird, you on the tequila binge and him dry as a boat in December. He just sits there, not even talking to me, with a cola or tea—that guy, drinking tea!—and stares at that damn booth." Jen nodded at the back half of the room where it was less a bar and more a restaurant tucked into a bar.

Carly turned and looked at the booth in question. Second from the corner, lit enough to eat but still have some privacy, it was the place Parker had told her he had feelings. It was the place she'd nervously admitted she did as well. It was the home of a three-hour conversation neither of them really remembered much of, other than the fact they came out the other side of it as something else. Something that became dating, then living together, then talking about a real future. And then it crashed to the ground. She looked away from the booth and downed the shot glass of agave nectar.

"Seriously, Carly." Jen refilled the same shot glass rather than replacing it with a clean one, leaving the bottle of 1800 Silver on the bar. "Get over whatever it is and either forgive him or cut him loose and move on. But don't do this limbo shit to him… Or to yourself."

"Really Jen, you're going to take that route?"

"Yeah, really. And I'm a bartender, which means I'm an underpaid over-schooled shrink and you should fucking listen to me."

Carly smiled at her, grabbed the bottle and glass and turned toward the aforementioned booth.

"I'll bring your wings and rings over when they're done."

"I don't want—"

"Shut up. If you want that bottle and think you're going to drive, you're going to put something in that gut to mop it up."

Carly shrugged her acquiescence and walked over to the booth.

CHAPTER TWENTY

Otto pulled onto the shoulder in front of the broke down FedEx truck and cut the engine. Climbing out of his service truck, Otto felt all fifty-four of his years in his knees, as his feet hit the hard blacktop of Highway 2, otherwise known as East 2nd when referring to the street rather than the US Route it truly was. Favoring his stiff left knee, aching from what he knew was only partially arthritis and mostly years of abuse, bruises and bangs on equipment, Otto reached the door of the FedEx truck and banged on it twice before opening it.

The empty cab was unexpected but didn't alarm him. He licked his front teeth with closed lips in thought, a twitch his wife loved to chastise him for, and looked around. He nodded at no one and decided Booker had most likely walked to the Kwik Trip he could see up ahead.

"That's fine. Don't need you in my way anyway."

Otto shut the door and went to work, deciding to check the engine before pulling out the equipment and running diagnostics. *Maybe it was something simple.* Unhooking the driver's side hood latch as he passed it, Otto walked around the front of the vehicle. He snarled when he smelled the diesel, and knew at the very least there was a cracked injector, if not several misfiring, causing power loss with possible fuel leaks. He reached the passenger side, flipped the hood latch, and heard a phone ringing.

Being six-four, Otto was used to being tall enough for just about anything, but not enough to see clearly into the truck through the high window. He pulled the door open, thinking Steve had left his phone in the cab when he hiked over for a snack. No phone.

"Steve?" He called out and looked down the side of the truck. He started to squat to look under the truck but knew his knee would never forgive him, so he backed up into the tall grass and weeds of the ditch and looked up and down the underbelly of the vehicle.

"Booker?"

He licked his teeth and spun around, realizing the ringing was behind him.

"Booker!" He couldn't see anything but a path of broken weeds in the marsh. He snarled and started following the trail in front of him. "What are you doin' out here, Steve?"

He walked fifty yards or so and found a patch of weeds stained red. He took a step back. He knew clay, and he knew what the grass looked like after he gut a deer during the fall bow hunt. This was blood. And too much of it to be any good.

"Steve!" He called with more urgency as the phone began to ring again. The sound was much louder than it had been at the truck. Closer. And he followed the chirping with his eyes until he came upon the Samsung laying face-up at the far edge of the bloody swath of grass. He took one step closer to read the screen and confirm what he already knew.

Yup, he thought. The screen declaring DOUGIE was calling meant it was indeed Steve's phone. He turned to walk back to the truck to call for help, not willing to deal with whatever had turned a medley of old dried grass and a fresh spring growth of weeds into a red wash of death.

He got two steps before he went down hard on his bad knee. Without time to even put his hands out in front of him, Otto face-planted and sent his top two front teeth into the tender flesh of his bottom lip.

"Mother—" He cursed as he pushed himself up, the

marsh wet enough to soak his knees and now hands with muddy brackish water. "What the hell?"

Otto looked around him for the culprit, expecting to find a root sticking out or some other such obstacle. He was not expecting the trio of very snake-like tentacles flicking hypnotically in the still water. Having chased his fair share of snakes as a child, he immediately knew that was not what they were, and pondered for a very brief moment if they were lampreys. He followed them from the tip backward, trying to find the end and lost them in a mass of knotted weeds and brambles.

Beyond them he saw a dark haired woman watching him and he jumped with surprise. He could clearly see from her bare collarbone up, and opened his mouth to warn her of the eels she was wading so close to.

She smiled.

Rather than causing him to believe there was a relaxed feminine need for him to save her, the jagged teeth she exposed immediately turned on his fight or flight—and he was unarmed and unable to properly fight his way out of this. Otto turned, ignoring the pain shooting through his knee, and sprinted toward the road. A handful of steps into a full run and he was taken down again, this time he turned in time to see it wasn't a root, but rather one of the black tentacles, which seemed to be attached to the lower half of the woman.

"What the fuck?" He pulled his leg away and tried to get up. Again a tentacle was wrapped around his leg and jerked him down. *She's fucking toying with me.*

He quickly slapped his pockets, hoping for keys or a pen or anything he could call a weapon. Finding nothing he quickly glanced around him, keeping her in his peripheral view the entire time.

She seemed to glide closer, and he noted there were

five black tentacles pushing through the weeds and pulling back toward her again, like a pulsing search of the marsh. Her silver eyes were unblinking. Her small nose almost appeared too small, like nothing more than a tiny bump with two holes. The black hair that framed her face seemed to cascade down her entire side, the tips becoming lost in the shallow water. Her mouth—

Otto was so fixated on her features, on the teeth he could see had bits of something, someone—*Steve?*—in them, that he didn't initially notice the other two tentacles were different.

Where the black eel-like appendages, which kept taking him down, were thick tubes of muscle about the width of his forearm, these new limbs were thinner, longer, and more dexterous. All of them were dotted on the underside with small round, bowl-like bits of flesh in a single line. They were close enough for Otto to note they were rimmed with a sharp saw-tooth ridge that looked to be more for latching on or tearing meat, than for chewing—he swallowed hard at the thought of either.

His gaze flicked from one to another, trying to keep them all in view. He watched as they alternately flexed and relaxed, in a motion he presumed was anticipation. The two new ones closed in and hovered in the air a foot away from him, the others remaining on the surface of the water if not just below it. Otto noted the two airborne tentacles ended with large flats of flesh, like a canoe paddle at the end of a long handle. He watched in horror as a hook of sorts unfurled and came away from the paddle, not unlike a thumb from a gloved hand. On the flat portion of the paddle, the black flesh was scratched and scarred from the tip of the claw.

Otto realized the limbs ending in paddles were

coming from her side, perhaps shoulders. *Oh god, are those her arms?*

He screamed, incoherently for a moment, and then began yelling, "Help!" In return he heard the engines roar past on the highway. He turned to see it was only fifty yards away, yet a distance he could not breech with sound only.

He felt a grip on his legs and looked down to see she'd come closer, wrapping her lower tentacles around his legs, one snaking its way up and around his chest, pinning his arms. She hovered like a slowly dancing snake in a basket in front of him for a moment, and then leaned in to look him straight in the eye. Otto jumped as the hooks of both paddled tentacles pierced his checks as she slapped them against the sides of his head. She hissed with delight behind a smile, opening her mouth to again expose the jagged teeth and tongue as black as her tentacle.

She bit down on his screaming mouth, tearing his lower lip away in a bloody kiss. He gurgled on his own gore but continued to scream. Still chewing his flesh, she turned and dove into the water behind her. She released his legs, holding him firm with the claw-paddle grip on his head, and used her lower tentacles to shoot through the weeds and marsh water toward the mouth of the river. As she hit the open water of the channel, dragging him behind, he slipped below the surface and stopped screaming.

They passed under the bridge and headed upstream. He watched an orange hue spread across the water above him as the day waned into dusk. Otto had fished the river many times at that time of day. He knew the tricks the light played on the tired eyes of fishermen and drivers alike. And he knew he'd just become nothing more than an illusion in the shadows of the setting sun.

CHAPTER TWENTY-ONE

Carly opened one eye, stretched and mentally berated herself for falling asleep on the couch again.

Fine, maybe I'm purposely avoiding the bed. Accept it and move on.

She accepted it, but acknowledged she needed a pillow or something on the couch so her neck wasn't always cranked into horrible positions. She reached blindly behind her for her phone, found it, and pushed the home button to light up the screen and reveal the time.

Instead of seeing the time right away, she saw two missed calls and a text from Donny. The text said simply, "Pick up." The clock in the upper left told her it was two o'clock in the morning. The voice mail had been left at midnight.

It's not a squid. God, I can't even believe I'm saying this. Not entirely squid? The circular wounds appear to be very similar to octopus. Octopus! Can you believe that shit? But wait for it… The neck and face wounds on the boating accident guy and the Mustang boy? Those could be squid, because they have a claw or tooth inside their whatevers, the suction cup things on their arms. Oh yeah, those are called arms, on squid and octopus, tentacles are actually the two longer arms on squid, again, with hooks inside. Christ. Is this some mutant cross-bred freshwater nightmare? The government do this? Should we call those boys from Mackinaw? Call me back… no. Just get down here first thing.

He didn't say goodbye and cell phones lacked that telltale click to let you know the call was ended, so when the dead air lasted more than three seconds, Carly knew he'd hung up. She replayed it. Twice.

"Fuck." She thought of all the crazy shit Granny Two Fingers had said. *Was this a mutant? Was the myth based on an actual creature?* She shook her head, rubbed her eyes, and tossed her phone to the couch cushion as she stood to go to the bathroom.

Washing her hands, she glanced in the mirror. Her black stick-straight hair fell halfway down her back, and was never knotted. It was the strangest blessing a girl could ask for. She could crawl out of bed at any hour and her hair would be fine. Her face on the other hand—mascara matted the lashes of her left eye together, eye liner was smeared underneath like pseudo bags of exhaustion, and a very prominent crease from the stiff piping edge of the unforgiving arm of her couch combined to give her the look of someone desperately in need of rehab. She leaned down and splashed her face with water, wiped it with the washcloth hanging next to the towel on the rack, and declared it good enough.

"Fucking squid women." She muttered as she made her way to the kitchen. Pulling open the fridge, she looked over the contents without actually seeing any of it and shut it empty-handed. She dumped the water glass on the counter into the sink, ran the water for a few moments to get it cold, and refilled the glass. Glancing at the Mr. Coffee in the shadows of the cupboard, she saw half a pot left from the morning, Carly admitted defeat, "Yup, I'm awake now," and pushed the button to turn it on and heat it up.

She took her water glass and went back to the couch to allow the coffee time to warm up. Crossing her legs on the cushion, she flipped through her notebook. Donny had said octopus, and squid, but he hadn't mentioned human—woman or otherwise—and she wondered if it wasn't just some crazy hybrid creature. Except they didn't live in fresh water, did they? And if it was, then that in itself was unusual. And Granny Two Fingers had been right about the cephalopod portion of the myth…

"Oh god. Half woman, half calamari? Really? How do I sell this to the chief?"

Going over the description she recalled from Granny and the notes she'd made, she started sketching. She'd never been good at drawing and cracked her laptop to search for myth references drawn by better artists.

CECELIA in the search engine returned the meaning of the name and several supposedly famous women she was unfamiliar with. Adding MYTH showed her the spelling correction and she started over.

CECAELIA.

She spent several minutes reading a handful of pages, only to dismiss them as role-playing or fan fiction for a variety of fantasy shows from Supernatural to Once Upon a Time. Adding MYTH afterward changed the search immediately and she shook her head at her mistake.

As she scrolled down the Google results, she opened pages in new tabs and left them there, gathering several before going to skim them and either bookmark them or close them. Her head began to swim with scattered bits of stories and tales and internet claims of authentic history. Some said they originated in Asian mythology or Native America folklore—to which Carly paused and thought that bizarre, as those people were separated by an entire ocean and centuries of discovery. She read of the bad wrap they'd gotten as sea witches, complete with magic to control the moon, tides and weather. And finally learning the term Cecaelia itself was new, only introduced in the last fifty years.

It was a lot of fantastical stories and claims. Too much. And none seemed helpful. She needed to find the right pages, the information that would bring the creature down. She needed a way to stop the attacks and accidents and bodies being chewed on by something that shouldn't even be living in the fresh water river to begin with.

She needed Parker.

She sighed, grabbed her phone and headed to the kitchen for coffee. It went to voice mail and she immediately redialed. Parker answered on the third ring.

"Everything okay, Hon?"

His voice sounded like he'd been in one of his lumberjack-snore deep sleeps, but his words showed her habit—both reaction and affection.

"Can you come over?" She hated needing him. It made her feel weak. But damn he was good at what he did.

His voice cleared and became louder. She imagined he'd sat up more panicked than necessary. "Carly? Are you okay?"

"I'm fine. Promise. Can you just come over?"

"You mean come home?" The hope was so obvious in his voice it made Carly actually feel a twinge of guilt.

"No. Not to stay. Just come by, and bring your laptop." She thought for a moment and realized she knew exactly how to get him there. "I have a scoop for you."

• • • • •

"Wait a fucking minute." He'd listened to her retell Granny Two Fingers' stories, and then watched her awkwardly summarize what she had found online. He held the cup of coffee in front of him, untouched, as his mouth had been open and eyes narrowed in disbelief since she'd first said Whore of the Gods. "Do you mean like the witch in Little Mermaid?"

"Yes, exactly! Oh my god, that's the perfect comparison. Ursula, right? Yeah, I think so, anyway. Top half is a woman, bottom half is an octopus, or squid, or both, I don't know. Granny said tentacles but didn't say which animal. And Donny was... well, confusing on about which critter was leaving marks on the bodies, maybe both. He questioned military hybrid."

Parker's eyebrow rose enough to move his hairline. "And you're buying this?"

"Are you?" She shrugged.

He looked at her without blinking for a few moments, took a drink of the reheated coffee, made a face and put it down on the coffee table. "Okay, for the sake of covering all our bases, let's look up everything we can on octopuses... octopi? What's the plural of octopus? Anyway... and squid. And Jesus Christ, I guess Ursula myths."

"Okay." She nodded and pulled her laptop onto her knees, as Parker opened his and waited for it to automatically connect to the wireless router.

Dueling laptops, Carly smiled at the peripheral view, not letting him see her notice it. *I kinda miss this.*

"Hey."

She looked up and realized Parker was watching her look out the corner of her eye. Carly was busted and dreaded what came next. "Yeah?"

"Do you have anything stronger than coffee?"

She nodded and retrieved him the last bit of the Patrón and a small glass.

"Where's your glass?" He held the tequila out for her.

"Nah, I'm good with coffee. Thanks." She turned back to her laptop but saw the look of approval. *I was never the drinker in this relationship anyway,* she thought and started sharing with him the screens she'd kept open.

An hour later they could have written a fairly convincing paper on the history of mermaids, cecaelia, octopus and squids.

"Nibiinaabe, eh?" He skimmed the screen of her laptop. They'd discovered it was faster than her reading it out loud. Whenever she found something good, she just turned it toward him so he could read it.

"It's one of the myth's Granny brought up, and the only thing I can find that's even close to a cecaelia in native lore, even though she's supposedly originates there."

"Why wouldn't they have stories and legends and—"

"Granny said, only the myths are in the books. She was real—"

Parker nodded and finished her thought for her, "And what do all children do with tales of the boogeyman? Do they advertise that shit? No. They whisper it around campfires and under blankets with flashlights beneath their chins. Myths are shared. Real monsters are kept secret."

"Jesus… you think she's real?"

"I think they believed she was." Parker swallowed the last of the tequila.

"We gotta get them to dredge the river. We have to find that thing and stop it, half human or not, it's killing."

"Isn't this the part in the horror movie where they talk to the survivor and get some vital piece of information?"

"We don't have any survivors…"

"Why didn't it hit open water? Why not go out into the lake? I mean, if it's really a—what was that called? A brief squid? It's the only fresh water squid but it's in areas like the Chesapeake Bay on the coast. This is really far inland for a coastal creature."

"Well, I'm guessing it's also bigger than the five inches that squid gets to." She shrugged. "But if there's *one* who lives in freshwater…"

"Then there's precedence. Jesus, Carly. Is this real?" He covered his face and rubbed his forehead as if disbelief was physical and he could wipe it off.

"I don't know, but something is, and we have to stop it." She closed her laptop. "I'm going to tell the chief we need to dredge, and I'm thinking maybe we should put a twenty-four hour watch on that cavern. Maybe it's coming back to there. I mean, if it was really trapped for that long and it's not jetting out into the lake to take off, I imagine it's still calling that home."

"Makes sense. But how the hell are you going to tell your supers about this? You know how crazy this sounds?"

"Oh I know. Not even a little bit crazy in a cute way. No, this is bug-fuck crazy. But I'm going to say the dredging is to find the other body from the fishing accident, which might not be an accident at all. Donny can back me up and say there's attack marks from something large in the water. We need to find the other body for the family, but also to figure out what we're dealing with. We'll just play dumb and pretend it's a fish." She used air quotes when she said *fish*.

"It might work." Parker put his laptop on the table.

"It has to."

CHAPTER TWENTY-TWO

"But is there any sign of it being human?" Carly looked over the printouts on Donny's desk—*his* research into all things octo-squid from the previous night.

"Not necessarily *human*, but there is sign of something very much *not* cephalopod."

"Yeah?" Parker had no notebook, no recorder. He had nothing but coffee, and red rimmed, but *wide* eyes as he listened intently.

Carly grabbed Parker's coffee and stole a sip before handing it back. Hers had been gone before they got out of the car at the morgue, and she figured he owed her at least a sip for letting him crash on the couch for three hours. Less than a night's rest, but more than a nap, Carly wasn't sure it would be enough to get either of them through the day and was hoping she could sneak a nap in at some point.

Donny turned to the heavier male body, the fishing accident. "See this here? On his lower pectoral and again on his thigh?"

They both nodded.

"The streaks, there, that almost look like lines in the flesh right before the missing tissue, those are from teeth dragging across there. Very sharp, very thin, very nasty teeth from the looks of these wounds." He looked up at them and held Carly's gaze. "Think walleye or pike teeth, those super sharp thin teeth. But worse."

"Worse? You ever been tagged by a walleye? That sucks pretty bad." Parker raised his eyebrows.

"Worse because they're longer, and tighter together. Like your worst childhood nightmare monster."

"But not human?" Carly tried to ignore the imagery creeping into imagination.

"*Not* human. But also not octopus or squid."

"So, more questions and no answers. Fuck." Carly sighed in exaggerated frustration and looked at the ceiling. "What do you have that we know for sure, Donny."

"The boating accident, the fishing accident, and now your caretaker," he pointed to the third table over, a sheet covering the body laying there patiently waiting for his attention. "All three show marks from whatever this is. Whether it's an octopus, a squid and a pike hanging out together like some crazy opening to a joke, or some fucked up mythological creature. It's definitely responsible for the marks on all three—circular suction wounds and teeth tracks."

"So we tell the chief it's a fish and get Fish and Game involved?"

Donny shook his head, "No, I like the other idea you had. We need to dredge to find the body and the *unknown* water animal responsible for these attacks. We start talking about octopus or squid and they'll lock us up. We mention the teeth and they're going to start thinking crazy shit about crocodiles up north."

"Croco—" Carly's eyes widened.

"No. We don't have crocks here." Donny almost smiled as he reassured her.

"Just some living myth chewing on citizens." Parker spoke and Carly watched Donny's expression promptly return to something much more grim.

• • • • •

"Whatcha got?" The chief of police, having shown up four hours after the dredging had begun, hollered from the riverbank at the two men in the boat currently pulling something up.

They shook their heads as it broke the surface of the

water. "Just another fishing pole. This one stuck to a log."
The Sheriff's deputy, borrowed for the manpower, pointed
at the heavy waterlogged chunk of wood sticking out of
the water.

The chief sighed, "What have you found so far,
Greene?"

"A couple dozen shoes, none matching that I know
of or with feet still in them. Several fishing coolers, which
oddly I would have thought would float, but if cracked,
open, or as in the case of one of them, shot through with
a small caliber, they sink. Some random crap—ball caps
and garbage. Oh and one pissed off sturgeon that almost
gave the Warden a heart attack. He's been on shore ever
since." She indicated the man to her right with the wet
pants and angry scowl on his face.

"Do we need to go further up the river?"

Carly shrugged and watched the various boats on the
water. The river was too small to bring in actual dredging
equipment, so they were lined up like soldiers dragging
weighted nets and rakes across the bottom hoping to snag
anything that may be hiding in the clay-colored water.
Divers had been suggested and she'd barely contained her
fear of lunch being served to the cecaelia. She suggested
the water was too stirred up and muddy to begin with to
make visibility even possible.

"Anyone go under there and scrape around in the
chasm?" The chief pointed upstream as if they could see
around the bend from where they had currently worked
their way to, near the mouth of the river.

"They raked it from outside." She nodded at her
superior but kept her attention on the boats. "They tried
to fill that in twice now, but the current is too much.
They're going to wait for the water to recede in a week or
so and then use the storm fencing to create a fake wall and

fill in behind that."

"No danger of the graves coming through."

She glanced at him, hearing the tone in his voice. "No sir. Once we've got this wrapped up, it shouldn't be a problem again. The plans are to fortify the entire bank along the cemetery and twenty yards on either side of it just to be sure."

"Good, because it's an election year and you know the mayor—"

"Is doing his damnedest to avoid this?"

He shot her a look that told her he thought about scolding her for tone, but the look softened and Carly knew he couldn't disagree.

"Hey, at least he gets points for offering to cremate the Indians from the mass grave." Carly squinted at movement in the water.

"*He* didn't. I suggested he do that to save face and maybe his seat."

Carly took a step forward and realized the chief had said something, "What? I'm sorry."

"Nothing. What do you see? What's wrong?"

She shook her head. "Nothing. I swear... I've been staring at this water for so long I'm starting to see shit in it."

"Fishermen claim that all the time, though usually closer to sundown."

"Sir!" A beat cop pulled from the street to walk the shore with a net hollered at the two of them.

The chief headed for the man without another word to Carly. "Whatcha need, Harris?"

Carly heard the officer say something about overtime, but tuned it out as Parker entered her peripheral vision.

"Anything to report?" He seemed sheepish about asking questions and Carly wondered if he was playing it professional because most of the police force and sheriff's department were on the scene.

She shook her head just as she saw movement in the water again. The barely perceptible slash of color, or lack thereof, was nothing more than a darker streak in the already dark muddy water. It moved toward the mouth of the river, approaching the boats. And then she watched in slow motion as it smashed into the side of the boat directly in front of her. The officer at the front of the boat squealed, was knocked off balance, and fell into those muddy waters.

Carly gasped an intake of air that tasted of shock. When she realized it was Mikey who had been thrown, her shock became fear, and she subconsciously grabbed Parker's arm next to her. In unison the two of them took several steps closer to the edge of the embankment. If it had been flush to the water here, she may have run in for him, but there was a four-foot drop from the shelf of the bank she stood on down to the edge of the water.

"Mikey!" She screamed, frozen where she was so she wouldn't slide off and join him.

She watched the dark streak in the water, afraid to lose it, and kept him in her peripheral. Rather than reach for the boat and try to pull himself out of the water, Mikey turned and swam for shore. Carly shook her head, brows furrowed in anticipation, as the black lines—*oh god, tentacles?*—passed between the boat and Mikey.

No, no, no, she thought. *Get in the boat.* Unable to voice her thoughts or why, she simply nudged Parker hard in the ribs and pointed to the black line in the water.

"Oh fuck. Is that—?"

The boat turned toward Mikey, quickly closing the distance between them and momentarily blocking Carly's view of whatever had been in the water. Mikey yelped and was suddenly standing, having hit the shallows, and running in that almost slow motion style of being in water or snow above your knees. He hit the shore and kept going, scrambling up the side of the hill and falling down in front of Parker and Carly, exhausted, scared, and out of breath.

"Are you okay?" Carly bent down, the worry in her making her heart race.

He shook his head.

"Sturgeon!" Another officer in a boat yelled and pointed.

Carly looked to see him referring to a large black shape as it slipped between two boats and left the river for the bay.

Mikey looked up at her, "Sturgeon?"

"That was, yeah." She nodded and felt Parker squeeze her arm.

Mikey sat up and she shot Parker a look that meant *later*.

"You wanna be done?"

"Nah. Just a stupid fish." He hopped off the ridge and climbed back into the boat waiting at the shore for him.

"That wasn't a sturgeon, Carly."

"What they pointed at *was*. It was much thicker and moved differently. They all saw it. It was a sturgeon. And that's a good thing."

"Yeah, but what hit the kid…"

Carly shook her head, "Was a different shape. Moved different. Was something else."

"Shit." Parker said it under his breath, but Carly heard it clearly and concurred wholeheartedly.

The chief walked back over. "This is your baby, Greene. You wanna call it or dredge it again? Maybe go out in the bay a little?"

She glanced behind her at the sun sitting low on the horizon. "We're almost out of daylight. We'll have them do a quick run on the way back to the vehicles and call it for today. And yeah, maybe the bay, but we'd need the bigger equipment for that wouldn't we?"

"Maybe. Remind me again why we're looking so hard for a boating accident vic?"

"Because of Larry and Debbie Race."

"Race?" The chief curled a lip at her. "From back in the 80s?"

"Yeah. If they would have accepted *accident* then, he would have gotten away with it. Until we have a body, an equally dead body, I don't know that Ullman wasn't killed by his friend."

"Okay, good point. I'll give orders to resume and do another full run in the morning." He turned and walked away like he always did before a conversation felt completed. She realized him doing so was his way of having the last word.

Carly took a deep breath, her heart finally back to normal with Mikey out of danger and the chief no longer asking questions. She glanced at Parker and wondered what she would have done if that had been him tossed into the water, and came to one solid conclusion. *I can't waste my life being angry at someone I can't stand to lose.*

"Should have been more fish in here." Gary Scott, the part-time Fish and Game Warden, scratched at the scruff he called a beard and interrupted Carly's thoughts.

"What?"

"There should have been more fish in here. A lot more. The eco-system is off." He looked at the water. "Between the spawn and natural movement in the river this time of year, there should have been a lot more... I'm going to look into this. Maybe the high water is to blame."

Or maybe something is eating all the lower life forms, Carly thought. She looked at Parker and realized he was thinking the same thing.

"What kind of animal are we looking for Detective?"

"Not sure, big pike maybe? Something toothy with enough mass to scare seasoned fishermen."

"A really big pike could scare the medium fish and eat most the small ones." He nodded to himself rather than Carly. "Yeah, I'll be back tomorrow."

"You going in a boat?" Carly didn't need to look to hear the sarcasm in Parker's voice.

"No. I'll stay on the sidelines with the journalists." He turned and left.

"Ouch."

"You had that coming." Carly started back up the length of shore toward the cemetery and the vehicles. The sun setting created ever-darkening shadows and she kept her eyes on the river as she walked.

CHAPTER TWENTY-THREE

Granny Two Fingers walked down the quiet street, as the sun slowly sank behind her, lengthening her shadow on the sidewalk. The neighborhood tribal members were all indoors for dinner at that time, leaving the porches absent of those who would see her.

Though she had often been accused of having young eyes, youthful hair, and even ageless skin, she knew she was *many* years beyond young, and would argue she was well into elderly. She could feel her age in her bones on a daily basis, but tonight, fueled by the importance of her mission, her steps were steady, her gait was sure. Even her arthritis seemed to be behaving. She was grateful for both the sneakers she had on her feet, and the walks she had been taking in them nightly to keep her knees and hips from stiffening. Satisfied, she walked to the end of Itasca Street, paused to check her breathing, and turned left as the pavement gave way to gravel.

Granny Two Fingers had stood when the detective left the previous day, watching her from behind the curtains in the living room. The moment the woman was out of sight, she started pulling out every book she could find that hadn't been printed by a press. She needed to read and re-read all the notes, notebooks, tomes and journals of her ancestors. She even flipped through cookbooks and recipe boxes for random information. She found only a few references and little to go on, other than a passage from a shaman and a small snippet from a midwife medicine woman. A full afternoon of going through everything the tribe had handed down to her and left in her care for situations just like this, had led to an exhausted evening with little sleep. Waking repeatedly, convinced she was hearing something, Granny felt barely rested the next morning as she resumed her search in the old pages.

After a brief nap and a small lunch, she'd decided to go to her father's house. Under the guise of bringing lunch to her younger brother, the current resident of said house, Granny excused herself having already eaten and went to the attic.

She found a strange sense of calm in the dust motes that floated in the afternoon light and recalled many an afternoon in the attic going over papers and lessons with her father and grandmother. She was taught the myths and the ways, the path and the pride. She was to carry it forward and protect what was left of their nation on this land. Most of the notebooks, journals, and ancient leather-wrapped pages had already been moved to her home when her father passed, but on the off chance something had been missed...

The smell of the attic, musty with a hint of brittle wood in danger of burning at the slightest spark, drew her deeper into the shadows and through older trunks and boxes that had seen better days. Tears came to her eyes when she found her grandfather's journal and she wondered why it hadn't been given to her. Though, wrapped as it was in old christening gowns and forgotten ceremonial dresses, she presumed it had been lost. It was the only helpful thing she'd found, and she tucked it into the folds of her shawl before heading back downstairs. She didn't want to worry her brother, and she didn't want to start anything that may or may not turn into a battle over who should have the journal. *If there's nothing in it, perhaps I'll give it to him to cherish.*

Before heading to her father's, Granny had looked through her things one more time. In doing so, she'd located ancient words in one of the books from her mother's grandfather. The pages spoke of three items—black, brown and orange, like the colors of the Nemadji—and included a phrase to be spoken to the moon. She nodded at the hidden instructions and clues she'd found in the book bound in birch bark and tied with braided cord. On it's own, the information wouldn't have felt pertinent or complete. But with the help of an unexpected passage in the newfound journal of her grandfather, regarding not a legend or myth, but rather a dream, she felt prepared.

The dream in question had wild rice, tobacco, and a small hand picked bunch of orange flowers with small green pods. He had called them swamp poppers, but Granny knew they were jewelweed, and while often located by water, they were also a cure for poison ivy, oak and sumac. In the dream, the ingredients—black, brown and orange—sat on a table while his granddaughter continued to reach for them. His granddaughter, Granny Two Fingers, would have been nothing but a beansprout of a girl at the time—barely more than six years old if the dates in the journal were to be believed. It would be decades later when she would need those things. And having the understanding to put the ingredients from one with the directions from another, she had gathered the necessities.

Granny wrote the ancient words for the moon on a piece of purple stationery one of her grandchildren had given her for Christmas and tucked it into her pocket. She grabbed her first-knife from the shelf, almost without thought and afterward decided it would be good to have with her. The knife had been the first weapon she made as a young girl. A sharpened agate formed a crude arrowhead tip and braided leather held it with straps to a short length of silver, which had once been the handle of an expensive hairbrush given to her mother on her wedding day. A pouch of tobacco, a small bag of wild rice, and her walking stick later, she was ready and had quietly left the house without locking the door.

Now, she slipped into the weeds on the side of the small dirt boat launch and pushed the canoe hiding there out into the water. A voice startled her as she stepped into the canoe. She turned to see a young girl walking back from the dead-end point with a child's pink fishing pole over her shoulder and an empty stringer by her side.

"Where are you going at night, Granny?"

Granny Two Fingers held her remaining index finger to her lips and whispered, "To put a secret back where it belongs."

CHAPTER TWENTY-FOUR

By the time everyone got back to the vehicles parked at the cemetery, the sun had completely set. Carly couldn't remember the last time she'd been near graves in the dark and was unnerved at how creepy the statues appeared. As everyone left for the day, the headlights passed over marble and polished granite, reflecting like quick flashes of the afterlife, and gave her chills she wasn't prepared for and unequipped to handle.

The entire day had taken its toll on her and she skipped the welcoming taunt of the oblivion promised by a shot or bottle at the bar, driving straight home instead. She sat in her car at the curb for several minutes, just breathing. As she went over everything that had happened in the last week, she kept returning to one thing. Yes, the idea of a mythological half-octopus on a feeding frenzy freaked her out. Yes, she still hated floaters more than any other body she'd been called to deal with. Yes, she was completely analytical and professional, but grossed out by the gore offered by fresh death and mutilated bodies. But it was Parker that kept her in the car, her mind spinning. It was thoughts of Parker causing the windows to fog, as her breathing threatened to become the labored gasps of panic.

Carly couldn't stop thinking about her reaction when Mikey was knocked from the boat and landed in waters. Waters which were suddenly not just muddy, but dangerous—if not life threatening. She couldn't stop reliving it as if it *had been* Parker. She couldn't get the taste of fear out of her mouth or stop her imagination from playing the worst possible outcomes on a loop. The bodies she'd dealt with over the past week flashed through her mind, though now each of them had Parker's face.

And she finally succumbed to the meaning behind her thought at the river.

If I can't stand to lose him, I'm not done with him.

She let that thought roll around for almost fifteen minutes. Then started the car, leaned forward, and wiped the condensation from the inside of the windshield with her palm, before heading to the hotel he'd been calling home since she'd kicked him out.

She stood by her decision to send him packing. She stood by her reaction in general that day. And whenever she found herself able to think of it with a calm, rational mind, she was almost proud of herself for taking the high road, for keeping her calm. Though most of the time she recognized it as being less about control and more plain old shock.

Parker had never expected her to be out at Wisconsin Point that day, just taking a drive for lunch and aimlessly ending up at the sand dunes there. In turn, Carly had never expected when she saw his car and walked over to it, that he wouldn't be alone. She never, in a million years, would have guessed she'd ever see *that* look on his face—guilt and shame and fear, all wrapped into one and coated with an out of place justification based on nothing but self-protection. She had truly believed he would *never* hurt her, *never* destroy her. And yet there it was, as she stood speechless in the sand outside his car and he looked up at her. The girl beneath him unaware of her presence.

She saw it every time she closed her eyes. She relived it every night, with her imagination tacking on pretend and presumed conversations, and previous encounters, and coloring in all the gory details she neither needed nor wanted. Every time she woke with a scream, or silently crying in her sleep, she felt a little piece of something inside her die under the pressure of pain. It felt like someone was actually reaching into her chest and physically squeezing her heart, causing her breath to pause, her throat to tighten, and her eyes to burn. She imagined it was very close to what someone felt who was being suffocated, and often lay there wondering when the darkness would just slip in from the edges to stop the pain. She cried uncontrollably at first—in the shower, in the car, even in public a couple times. She'd ended up having to take some vacation days just to get a grip on how to hold it all inside and pretend to be okay, to be able to function without crying or screaming—or, whenever he came around, swinging blindly hoping to hurt him in some physical way she knew would never make up for the emotional damage he'd done.

What he had done was unacceptable. But maybe, just maybe, it was forgivable.

They'd never know if they didn't deal with it. They'd never know if they didn't try. And she needed to know, one way or other. She needed closure. Either they came to an end, or she let go of that day. Him or his actions, one of them had to go away. The other would survive the victor. She hoped it would be him.

She held her hand up to knock on his hotel door, the flickering yellow bug lights making slight buzzing sounds and reminding her of every bad horror movie she'd ever seen. After several seconds she put her hand down and stared at the door, wishing she could see through it. Wanting to know what he was doing. Was he in pain? Was he suffering as well? His playful banter and attempts to make her smile in the past few days had been above and beyond his attempts over the last few months. She found it was easier to be around him, but it still somehow pulled every scab off and refreshed her nightmares.

Carly raised her hand again, determined to take a step

forward, one way or the other. She held her hand still, hovering just below the brass numbers 4-3 screwed to the door. When a moth landed on her hand, she blinked, realizing she'd been standing still that long. She flicked it away and brushed her hand through her hair, much like a young man would in a movie theater if he'd been caught making a move and needed to make it look like he was doing something else. She sighed, her chest hurt. She put her hand in her pocket as if to hide it in shame for not being able to follow through.

As she turned she saw Parker's older Cadillac parked next to her car—not in the greatest of shape, but still his pride and joy in its mildly faded 70s bronze. The windows appear almost tinted in the moonlight and she couldn't remember if it had been there when she pulled in. The driver's side window rolled down on its loud, jerky motor and she realized he'd either just pulled in or stayed in his car when she'd parked hers.

"I was wondering how many times you were going to *not* knock before you did." Parker leans into the moonlight, holding back a smile. "Never did knock, did you?"

Carly shook her head, feeling the heat of tears well in her eyes.

"Do you wanna talk?" Parker's expression became one of concern.

She shook her head again, trying to find the words. Trying to express her pain at both what he did and where they were now. She tried to convince her voice and mind to work together but got nothing but a loud swallow for her efforts.

"I see…"

"Come home." She finally managed to say something, and it was enough. She'd used the term "home" and knew he would know exactly what that meant. She turned away and got into her car, only realizing she was holding her breath as she let it go after leaving him in her rearview mirror.

CHAPTER TWENTY-FIVE

Granny Two Fingers slipped down the shoreline, the canoe slicing the water as she gently pushed her way along with a single paddle. The moonlight reflected off the still waters of the bay, as she worked her way around the Allouez Bay Channel, gliding between the abandoned grain elevators on her left and the end of Wisconsin Point on her right. As she passed the peninsula she knew marked the bird's eye line to the old burial grounds, she bowed her head and prayed for the dead who had been moved, those still in slumber, and any who may have been lost in between.

The lights of Superior's East End, and even those of Duluth across the water, caused an artificial glow in the sky. As she turned inward at the last outpost of elevator docks and headed for the mouth of the river, she blocked out those lights and the traffic around her. She focused her breathing, her intention, on nothing but the target. Glancing from the reflection to the moon proper, she thought of her father.

"I wonder, which of your Old Ones are aware their whore has been freed? Which will come knocking when her scent travels through the current to the farthest reaches of myth and man?" Granny sighed. She knew it was not the moon she spoke to, though it would appear so to the outsider.

When her grandfather died, Granny Two Fingers— who at that point in her life was only known by her given name, Pearl—had spoken to no one *other* than the moon for almost a month. She had spent so many of her early summers with her grandfather, and her room in his house had the perfect southeastern view, that the moon had often lulled her to sleep after her grandfather said his goodnights. She equated him with the moon for many years after. And when she went up against the wolf that took her fingers, it was her grandfather's spirit she begged for help, as she laid bleeding on the snow, watching the moon cross the sky. When her father died and the responsibility of the legends or lore were passed to her, when even the Fond du Lac reservation in Cloquet— though mostly run like a business with a board rather than a tribe with a chief—nodded to her as the current power for Wisconsin Point, she accepted the duty under a full moon. She and the moon went way back. It had always been equated to her grandfather. And it was her grandfather she addressed now, not the beautiful moon who listened in on her whispered words.

"I found your separate pieces and put them together. Words and weapons, in the form of black, brown and orange magic. I know to speak the words. I know to offer the colors. But I know not how to trap her again. Are your tricks for her slumber to give me time to bury her? Or did you find a way to destroy her should she ever escape? I wish I had your council. I wish you had told me what I needed, when you foretold this day would come."

Granny blinked and glanced at East 2nd as she passed underneath the bridge of the Nemadji. To her left she saw a FedEx truck and mechanic's service vehicle on the side of the road, no lit flares or any movement to indicate people at the scene. To her right, the Kwik Trip's bright lights seemed heavy with insects and Granny wondered how close the mayfly season was. The muddy river looked like a long red snake stretched out in front of her. Police tape floated past her, presumably torn from the branches and bushes along the side of the river, based on the strips still flicking like yellow tongues in the light breeze.

"I remember your words. I remember your last breath.

Smelling of cinnamon tobacco against doctor's wishes. I remember the look in your eye, straining silently for me to understand the importance of what you were saying. *Be prepared,* you said. *For it will fall to you to take the heart of darkness.*" Granny shook her head, "I always did find the poetic speak and riddles of the old ways to be tedious. I'm not a hero who needs to prove her worth to take down the monster. I'm an old woman, charged with protecting the land and legends from both man and myth. And I need your help, grandfather. Oh moon of mine, send for his spirit and bring me guidance, wisdom and a steady hand."

The curve of the river snaked left then right and she turned the paddle in the water, dragging the wide flat end behind her to slow the canoe. Even in the shadows she saw the darkness of the cavern. She pushed the canoe to the shore right after the chasm, the area often used for parking at the cemetery. An overturned backhoe lay on its side, but otherwise no other people or equipment could be seen from the shore. Using her walking stick, she stepped from the canoe to the muddy flats. Her sneakers were sucked down with a slurping sound at each step, as she followed the edge and made her way back to the wide opening under the overhand of bank.

Ducking to step inside, she almost lost her balance when the bottom vanished beneath her feet on the second step. She faltered for a moment, she caught herself and realized it had been dug out like a pool inside, and she continued though it was waist deep.

"Hello, Gete-Oga. I bring you offerings and beg to hear your tales." She held the tobacco and rice out in front of her with her good hand, the other hand gripping the walking stick as she carefully waded to the opposite side where she could make out a ledge and movement.

The tips of several tentacles dangled in the water and flicked. Following the sound and focusing in the dim light, Granny saw the cecaelia lying on its side on the ledge, propped up as if on an elbow—but the upper limbs were not human arms as she expected. They were long tentacles ending in flat pads like a squid's, but with the addition of sharp looking thumb-like claws. Gete-Oga smiled and the moonlight revealed two rows of wicked looking teeth—sharp, thin, and tightly crammed into the space provided in such a manner that several overlapped. Wicked as her mouth appeared, the silver eyes watching Granny didn't seem evil. Didn't seem spooked or worried. They seemed only to watch her intently, as if filled with a gentle inquisitiveness. A curiosity left to imagination for over five hundred years.

Gete-Oga hissed and grabbed the sacks from Granny's outstretched hand. "Brave girl."

CHAPTER TWENTY-SIX

The knock at the door could only be Parker, and Carly wondered if that moment was her chance to change her mind. Instead of even giving the thought a second to solidify, she walked to the door and opened it with a forced half-smile.

"You know, you still have a key. You could have just come in."

"I didn't want to push my luck." He spoke with hesitation in his voice and she noticed the computer bag hanging off his shoulder and the small suitcase he'd taken with him.

"Shut up. Did you eat yet? I'm starving and just tossed a lasagna in the oven."

"A lasagna?" He stepped inside and she shut the door behind him. "What if I'd have said no? What if I hadn't come until tomorrow?"

"Then I would have lunch for a week."

Parker smiled and watched her. She wondered what he was looking for and felt her stomach flip in a strange nervousness reserved for first dates. This was not a first date, but it may be the beginning of a new cycle. Carly couldn't find any words to make the awkward silence go away.

Parker finally did, "I'm going to put my clothes away."

Carly realized he was still standing by the door like a salesman with a suitcase at his side. "Okay, but don't get too comfy. You're home, but you're grounded to the couch for now, okay?"

"Fair enough." He turned and disappeared down the hall.

Carly heard the sliding of the closet door and rustling

of hangers. She listened intently to the almost silent scraping of drawers pulled out and pushed back in. Parker returned before she'd moved from her position near the door.

"That was quick." She tried to fill the empty air and realized it was equally hollow small talk.

"I didn't have all that much with me." He visibly sniffed the air, "But I am hungry."

"Good." Carly blinked and snapped herself out of her daze. "You're in charge of the garlic bread. You do it better than I do anyway." She indicated the loaf and tub of pre-whipped garlic butter on the counter.

"What time are we meeting back at the cemetery to start dredging again?" Parker pulled the long serrated bread knife from the block on the counter.

"We're not. Apparently, Game and Fish said without any signs of life, it's a waste and they're going to go into the bay and inlets where the boat was found and work over there tomorrow instead." She furrowed her brow as she realized she was talking as if life was just business as usual. "But I don't want to talk about work, okay? Not now. I'm gonna hop in the shower and wash today off me. I'll be out before the lasagna is done."

She hurried down the hall and hoped it hadn't appeared to Parker as if she were running away from him. Carly slipped into the bathroom and shut the door, leaning against it and shutting her eyes. She felt the precursor signs begin—eyes growing warm, throat constricting, chest squeezing—and took several deep breaths to try and prevent the panic attack that generally led to crying fits in the shower. She counted to ten and continued to breathe deeply.

In the nose, out the mouth.

She finally felt her heart rate come back down and

stood up straight. *What the hell is wrong with me?* She shook her head and looked directly across at the medicine cabinet mirror above the sink. She barely recognized her reflection. The woman in the mirror had long black straight hair that shined like it had been either oiled or brush a thousand times, neither of which she'd ever done. Her mother had always referred to her eyes as golden and her father still called them amber—but she claimed they were just brown. The skin tone was a light copper, thanks to the native blood in her veins, and the skin itself had always been smooth and mostly blemish free. As a whole, she looked okay.

But if you looked longer at those eyes, you'd see the pain hiding in the flecks there. You'd see the stress from the week pulling the lids lower than normal. And you may even notice the haunted look she tried so very hard to mask.

Carly peeled her clothes off, leaving them inside out and in a heap as if she were a teenager without a care. Pulling the shower on, because it was always in the same spot for the perfect temperature, she put her fingertips in the falling water and waited for it to heat up.

This is ridiculous. It's not a stranger or a first date. It's not like we haven't seen each other for weeks or months, we work together as much as he can finagle it. So why am I so nervous? What do I have to be nervous about? I have nothing to prove. That's all him. All on him.

Carly stepped in the shower and turned the dial up a touch, suddenly not wanting the same temperature she's always used. Suddenly needing to scald her skin and ground herself before she went out to face him. She shampooed her hair, applied conditioner, and then used the body wash on her bath scrunchie, scrubbing hard enough to exfoliate more than skin and wondering if she could wash pain down the drain. She rinsed the conditioner and stood there, eyes closed, head tilted up while the water continued to pour down her hair and stream down her face.

She dreaded the conversation that needed to happen. But Carly knew, from all the internet searches she'd done and "a friend of a friend" questions she'd asked of the station shrink, they would *have* to openly discuss what had happened. She'd have to ask questions—as much detail as she could stomach—because no matter how bad or graphic it may become, the truth would be better than whatever nightmares her imagination would conjure up. And he would have to answer, whether it hurt her to hear or not, whether he wanted to relive it or not. For them to get past this, first they would have to actually go *through* it.

Carly opened her mouth slightly and took a deep breath, trying to feel every drop of water touch her skin. She attempted to live in the moment, rather than the pain of the past or the what-ifs of the future. She found if she tried hard enough, she could imagine herself standing in a waterfall somewhere else. Somewhere far from unwelcome conversations and living myths.

She pushed the shower knob in to cut the water, *I guess my domestic waterfall will have to do for now, but I may very well put in for a real vacation somewhere when we're done with this crap.*

CHAPTER TWENTY-SEVEN

"Mother of myth, I know you're not a monster." Granny Two Fingers had slowly approached the ledge after Gete-Oga had snatched the bags with her paddle-claw hand. Standing a few feet away—Granny's walking stick leaned against the ledge while her hand gripped the handle of her first-knife in her back pocket—she stroked the tentacles hanging over into the water as she tried to sooth the creature.

Granny noted the upper body, the human torso in perfect proportion to a real woman, was not quite covered in skin but rather a smooth water-flesh like an eel—just a much lighter color to confuse sailors and lonely fishermen into believing it was human flesh. Up close she could understand how easily it would be believable, and imagined at a distance there'd be no question it was a human female.

The lower body, consisting of the tentacles Granny was calmly petting, was black like tar but shimmered as if the tentacles had been oiled. Even the portion out of the water was smooth to the touch with a permanent shine to it. Granny's eyes followed the length of the visible tentacles, and she presumed them to be ten to twelve feet long—making it easy for the creature to strike out before her prey got too close and saw the truth.

"You were made monster by association, but you yourself are just a victim. I know this. I respect this." Granny continued to stroke the tentacle but took in the other details of the myth in front of her.

The creature's hair framed its face in jagged lengths and random curls, which may have been nothing but cowlicks in what was actually a fur of sorts rather than hair, but it all made it look like a stylist had layered it and added to the human facade. The mane continued down Gete-Oga's back, and Granny realized it was not freely flowing from the skull only, but seemed to come out of the skin all the way down the spine, making it appear longer than it actually was and much more like a horse's mane than a luxurious human head of hair.

The eyes, the silver eyes, blinked at her like twin moons shimmering in a cloudless night. The lack of pupil in the center was the only thing that would give away the appearance of a striking young woman. The natural moisture levels in the eyes made it look like the creature was on the verge of tears and gave her an almost innocent appearance.

"You were designed to do exactly what you do. And even though I have pity for you, you're *not innocent*, Gete-Oga. No. I won't lie and say that. You've taken lives since you broke free. And I know you've released monsters, your seed, on man in the past. I know you've created nightmares that you've loved, though they've gone on to scare, haunt, attack or kill menfolk."

Granny carefully kept tabs on the creature's expression, and the movement of any of her limbs. She watched the two arm-like appendages coming from the shoulders, and what appeared to be a total of six tentacles from the waist, or rather, five and the remnants of what was once a sixth but was now a stub tipped with heavy scarring from a distant battle. Granny held back a smile at the possibility her own ancestors had done the damage while trapping her so long ago.

The ancient creature seemed complacent but watchful. While Granny spoke, she noticed its eyes often appeared sad or upset. Its breathing caught several times when Granny mentioned her offspring and sins.

The reflection of the moon edged its way into the

cavern as it set. Spreading closer and closer to Gete-Oga and Granny. Granny Two Fingers smiled, as the silver ripples came into her peripheral view. Perhaps her grandfather's spirit had come to help.

With a human torso—though flat-chested rather than voluptuous as the drawings would all suggest—Granny had half expected it would speak and thus be able to answer questions. Instead it seemed to understand what she said, but was not able to communicate in the same manner. Grunts and clicks were the best it could do and Granny had no idea how to interpret them.

Granny pulled the purple paper out, wondering if Gete-Oga would understand those words, and fearful the creature would know what she was doing. She had translated them to English from Ojibwa, hoping to hide their meaning and intent from a creature who had been locked away long enough to have never heard the language. Having given the black and brown to Gete-Oga already, Granny put her other hand in her pocket to wrap around the jewelweed for a moment, smashing them in her fingers and pulling her hand free but full of plant juice. Unfolding the paper, Granny Two Fingers cleared her throat.

"Under moon of silver light, in the silence of the night, flowers crushed upon her heart." She glanced and saw no reaction in Gete-Oga. "By the sun of morning light, with the passing of the night, oldest mother now departs."

Granny felt silly for a moment. It sounded like a child's rhyme. A horrible child's rhyme about a mother leaving—though Granny knows *leaving* in this sense is a euphemism for dying. She shudders at the absurd morbidity of it, but then she remembered Ring Around the Rosie was a child's rhyme about the Black Death, because that's how information is passed down. We pass knowledge to the children by making it a game. A game they'll hopefully remember as adults. *Ask any of them, they know the pockets are full of posies*, she thought and repeated the verse, twice.

The moon's reflection crept closer, crossing the threshold of the ledge Gete-Oga lay upon and shining on a small pile of weeds matted around a torn flannel shirt. In the center was an egg. A large, muddy brown, impossible to miss, egg.

"That's why you stayed in here rather than leaving for open water." Granny Two Fingers tucked the paper in her pocket and retrieved her first-knife, while her other hand reached for her heavy walking stick.

"I wonder," She kept eye contact with the creature rather than letting it see her stare at the truth hidden in the shadows behind her and revealed by the moon. "Is it old or have you been visited. Is it even alive inside or has it rotted and petrified with age?"

"You know, the monsters have all been beaten. Your children, they've all been sequestered to myth and legend and fairy tale. They are nothing but stories to scare children with only a handful of adults who know the truth. And I need you, the secret of you, to remain safe and hidden. I cannot have your seed out, not even one of them, to make everyone question everything they've ever believed…"

Granny tilted her head and held the creature's gaze tight. In one fluid motion, she raised her walking stick and threw it in the general direction of the egg. She was not hoping for a perfect javelin toss or even to spear the shell purposely, but if she could just hit it, the weight of her cane should be stronger than shell unless it was petrified. The walking stick flew past Gete-Oga before the creature had a chance to realize what was going on, and smashed into the egg, hitting it awkwardly and rolling off the ledge into the water.

A crack quickly traveled in an oblong path in the muddy brown shell, and the piece—slightly larger than Granny's hand—broke free from the rest and slid off the egg. Granny watched as Gete-Oga turned in time to see a pale mucus ooze out the wound in the shell.

"It *was* alive." Granny exhaled relief knowing she'd damaged it. She lowered her stance in the water, studying her body and prepared herself, still watching the egg to see what may fall out of it beyond the mucus meant to keep it alive inside.

The creature screeched at the sight of her offspring leaking out onto its nest of weeds and borrowed flannel, and snapped her attention to Granny. One arm-like tentacle shot out and wrapped around the old woman, pulling her off her feet and suddenly dragging her through the water toward Gete-Oga.

Granny had known the repercussions when she threw the walking stick, but she wasn't going to go down without a fight. She'd come with tricks and she would use them all. From beneath the tight embrace of the creature's tentacle, she wiped her first-blade across her palm and coated the sharpened agate with the plant juices left there from squeezing them in her pocket. Once applied, she adjusted her grip on the knife to ensure a better chance of stabbing the creature without her only remaining weapon being knocked away.

Gete-Oga slid off the ledge into the water as she pulled Granny close. Granny Two Fingers was brought to within inches of the creature's face by the tentacle, as she felt several others under water wrap around her waist and legs. The creature hissed through nightmare teeth and opened her mouth, showing Granny a tongue as black as a moonless night.

Granny was afraid the creature's intent was to rip her throat out with those horrible teeth and end her before she could even strike the thing she'd come for, though a victory for the monster inside the egg being stopped could be enjoyed, it wasn't enough. She prepared to jab the knife forward, hoping to stab where the heart should be if the insides matched the pseudo-human torso. The creature held her just far enough away that swinging or stabbing would not make contact and would give up the weapon. She had to wait until the last moment.

Gete-Oga hissed several times, with angry sounding clicks in between, and Granny realized she was being lectured or scolded in a tongue she didn't understand.

"I'm sorry. I truly am. I only meant to trap *you* again, not hurt you. But I *cannot* let your children loose. I can't."

A tentacle came up out of the water and slapped Granny in the face. She felt the small suction cups on the underside flex against her flesh in that instant of contact and tear away flesh as it returned to the murky water. The arm-like tentacle that had wrapped around Granny and pulled her close, released slightly and readjusted its location, moving up toward her neck. The creature cried again as it raised her into the air, holding her above the water and Granny saw it was crying from those silver eyes. She braced and knew a mother's rage was imminent. But this wasn't just a mother, this was the oldest mother. And Granny had no idea what that rage may look like, so she needed to be prepared at the first sign of a chance to strike.

As Gete-Oga lowered Granny, swiftly and unexpectedly toward the water, Granny flailed and swung out with her first-knife. She felt nothing but air on two passes but then the blade suddenly met with resistance and Granny tightened her grip while pulling the knife free and swinging it again in the same direction.

Granny hit the water flat on her back, slammed against the surface by an angry creature, and was pushed down into the muddy depths. She kicked and continued to swing the blade around. Gete-Oga pulled her up, glared at her with tear-filled eyes, screeched again with a rage that shook the small cavern and caused bits of clay to fall from the ceiling. The creature pushed Granny back into the water, but not as deep, keeping her near the surface and watching the fear wash across the woman's face.

She's going to drown me. Granny Two Fingers realized what Gete-Oga was doing. She wasn't going to bite her, maybe not even eat her. Because the creature was *older* than the white men who had come and settled here. Unable to communicate, Gete-Oga was still familiar with the old ways of the tribes who came before those white settlers. Granny understood that Gete-Oga knew being killed and not even eaten was an insult to the warriors of old. But Granny Two Fingers wasn't a warrior. And the tribe had evolved while Gete-Oga had been trapped in the riverbank.

And Granny was really okay with not being eaten.

She reached out of the water and shoved the point of her first-blade into the center of the creature's chest. She smiled, noticing the moon behind Gete-Oga's snarled face and imagining her grandfather's spirit watching her triumphantly. The creature howled, likely in pain but possibly thinking the grin was for her, and wrapped tentacles around Granny's body under water.

She felt them tighten on her legs and waist. Granny Two Fingers found it difficult to hold her breath, as her midsection was squeezed. Her legs were under great pressure for a moment, and then she felt an intense burning sensation followed by coldness and knew they'd been torn free. She felt the twisting of her midsection, and heard her bones cracking in a strange far away echo under the water. She felt her strength fade as her lungs started to burn from holding her breath.

As the moon began to fade and darkness crept into her vision, Granny Two Fingers thanked her grandfather for showing her the egg. She'd done as she should. She'd stopped the monster spawn from escaping. Hopefully the wound was life threatening—between the children's rhyme and the jewelweed, she could hope. She exhaled, closed her eyes, and waited to be welcomed by the crows and cranes of her ancestors.

CHAPTER TWENTY-EIGHT

"Just because it's a good story, a scoop even if you'd like to call first on the scene for murder and mayhem and insanity a scoop, doesn't mean you can tag along. You know the chief gets pissed and I get in trouble, and not for nothing, you've been right there all week. Constantly within at least my peripheral vision if not earshot of investigative work." Carly pushed the remaining bits of scrambled egg around her plate, separating them like a child trying to make it look like they had finished their meal.

"Murder? Is it murder when it's an animal?"

Of course that's all you heard, Carly wasn't surprised but tried to hide her annoyance, fearing it nothing more than a hangover emotion from the night before. "You know what I mean."

"Will you fill me in as much as you can when you can?" He swallowed the last of the coffee in his cup.

"Don't I always? And today will be a boring catch-up with paperwork kind of day, unless something else fucking happens... and I'm pretty sure we could both use a boring day so we're not hoping for more mayhem."

Parker nodded, "Cool. I'll be down talking to Donny for most of the morning, then I'm heading out to Allouez. I'm going to see if they're doing anything special to rebury their dead or are honestly interested in just scattering cremated remains. I can cover that, it's a good human interest piece in the middle of the nightmare."

"Just... just stay out of the way today, okay? And *away* from the water." Carly felt a chill run up her spine as the idea of him being tossed in the water went through her mind again.

"Fine. I'll be a good boy. I promise."

Carly started to reflexively reach for his hand on the table and veered to the center, straightening the salt and pepper shakers and hoping he hadn't caught her initial intention. She held her breath, waiting to see if she'd been busted, and thought about the previous evening.

The lasagna and garlic bread had been nice, but a thick expectation hung in the air and stained the calm with awkward silences. After dinner, their first attempt at a talk about his transgression and their current situation in general hadn't gone well at all. He was still very defensive, and she was still very hurt. Carly realized now, in the light of day, they may have to accept those things and try to work past them on the way to dealing with the other portions.

She constantly struggled with the idea she had any right to be angry or demand anything of him—after all, they weren't married. But he'd reassured her before and now again when it mattered, by living together they had committed to each other and yes, she had every right to be upset. Unfortunately, right or wrong didn't matter, and she'd only managed to ask a couple questions regarding the girl before she couldn't handle it anymore and excused herself under the guise of exhaustion.

She had gone to bed but sprawled across the blankets, rather than climbing under them. Carly threw his pillow—his scent still clinging to it—off the bed and lay diagonally. She stared at the ceiling for almost three hours, the sliver of light from the bathroom giving just enough illumination to create shadows she could manipulate with her imagination—like a child looking at clouds on a sunny day. About the time she thought of sneaking out to grab her laptop and get some work done, the steady sound of his snoring began to drift through the house. She smiled. It didn't matter where he slept, when he finally fell asleep he did it hard and could snore in almost any position. The rhythmic sound of familiarity was enough to lull her and she quickly drifted to sleep. Her alarm waking her in the same position.

"How bad was the couch?"

"You know, not as bad as you'd think. But it's my turn to get a shower." Parker stood and put his plate by the sink and his mug by the coffee pot, before disappearing down the hall to the shower.

She watched his actions and noted the sluggish movements, which replaced his normally very purposeful but fluid actions. She'd once referred to it as militant grace, as she watched him tie his shoes with sudden stark movements you could imagine being done to music. The sluggish approach meant he hadn't slept any better, despite his forced smile and purposefully lilted voice.

She put her dish next to his on the counter and reached for the faucet. "Nah, he can do them." Carly grabbed the small yellow note pad they kept on the kitchen counter for groceries and such, flipping it to a clean page, and left him a note.

Thought about scalding you, decided to be nice. Dishes are yours. ~ C

• • • • •

Carly could feel the rest of the department looking at her as she sat behind the desk she hated. She had almost finished the write-ups for the fishing accident and the caretaker, sprinkling her reports with field notes and specifics she'd gotten from Donny, and including his reports in the final binder. It had been the longest four hours of her life and she needed a break.

From her position in the back corner, her back to the wall, no one could see her computer screen and she took advantage of it. Leaning on her hand and staring intently, appearing to be working, she watched old Bugs Bunny cartoons on YouTube with the sound muted. Normally she would at least smile, if not laugh, but she was simply too drained mentally to enjoy it. Instead, she used it as a brain wipe, just meant to allow her to wander among the bright colors and outrageous antics of talking animals that often wore clothing.

She knew they'd have dredged the edge of the bay by now. From the mouth of the river and south, sweeping through and past the swampy area the boat had been found in. The lack of her phone ringing, even from Mikey with updates, meant they were finding more of yesterday's version of nothing.

The thought of Mikey reminded Carly of the young officer being tossed in the water the day before, and again brought her to the horrible visions of it being Parker instead. She wasn't sure they'd be able to fix their relationship, but she had hope and that was something. They may never be what they were, but they could be something else, something new, and still be stronger than most other couples. Maybe.

She blinked and looked at the screen, watching with genuine fascination as Bugs Bunny's rabbit hole floods because of the river next to it, and he floats up and out of it while asleep, remaining curled up and unconscious as he drifts down the river. Carly shook her head. *Wow, floaters everywhere.* She closed the browser and went back to the photo download file on her computer, pulling up the thumbnails to pick the best to print and put in the file.

The phone ringing on the desk actually startled Carly, though it was almost lost in the sounds of the office and muted underneath two file folders. She pulled it free and answered it without looking at the screen.

"Greene."

"Hey Carly, we got another one. Abandoned FedEx truck. Guess where..." Ben's voice sounded annoyed but she knew he was using this whole case as a giant lesson for all the street cops.

"Thank god." She hopped up, glad to be busy rather than flicking in and out of a continued cycle of productive paperwork and worrisome overthinking, and then felt bad because someone was most likely dead, eaten, and possibly missing forever but she was happy to call them a distraction.

CHAPTER TWENTY-NINE

"How did we not see this yesterday?" The chief of police appeared less than happy to be called back down to the river. Especially after he'd released everyone and declared it pointless to continue only an hour beforehand.

Carly had known the chief long enough to know what his anger was really about. It wasn't the idea of more missing, probably dead victims. It wasn't because they hadn't found anything. It was that they had seen this in plain sight, and he was afraid of looking like a fool. If it were perceived by the public they hadn't done a thorough enough job, it would reflect on the mayor and the election and subsequently his own job. *Bigger cases always made him bitchy*, Carly thought.

"I'm sure we *saw* it. We just didn't connect it to the others because it was on the road." Ben tried to be logical and gave Carly a look, begging her for some assistance.

"That's logical, Chief. We were concentrating so much on the water—"

"Well, now *those* boys need to come *over here* and do this whole section." He indicated the collection of small boats gathered at the mouth of the river, flicking his finger like a magic wand and then swirled it around him. He stood knee high in heavy marsh grasses and muddy stagnant water between the trucks and the bridge, and swung his arm to point beyond the trucks to the south.

"Make a triangle, from the Allouez park," Carly saw where the marsh met civilization. "To the mouth of the river and all the way up to the highway."

He turned to walk back up to his vehicle, his waders making horrible slurping noises. Turning back at Carly, his expression told her to be careful. "Do not call me again unless there's a body. People keep seeing me where there's nothing to show for our efforts and then the mayor is answering for us finding nothing with a story that won't die and botched re-election."

"No problem. We have enough people to search this section of the bay. Go."

"Greene," he squinted an eye at her.

Carly knew the look. "Reports are almost done and will be on your desk by tomorrow." She knew he understood the promised time frame was as good as claiming the check was in the mail but it was standard answer and accepted across the board at the precinct.

He nodded and walked away, forcefully pulling his feet free of the mud with each step.

"What's with him?" Ben watched the chief walk away. "The silt and mud aren't that sloppy over here."

"Oh, you never noticed? On land, the chief is a shuffler, never picks up his feet. He can snowshoe like a fiend if he needs, but this is probably making him crazy." She smiled and turned toward the marsh, looking at the path cut through the weeds from the two trucks on the highway to what looked like the location of the attack.

While the high water, and current it automatically generated, had attempted to *clean* the area, the blood spray and spatter was still evident on the taller pussy willows and cattails. "How many we got, Ben? And where the heck is Mikey?"

"One driver in each truck according to FedEx and the repair shop. Chief was talking like one killed the other, like he seems to think with the missing body from the boating *accident*, but I sense you have other ideas. As far as manpower, we've got six street cops, three part-timers from the warden, and two sheriffs, oh and one of Donny's deputies up on the shoreline chatting it up with the warden himself." He ticked the men off on his fingers.

"As far as Mikey, he went with the Donny to help him with something."

Carly looked at the shoreline on the other side of the bridge, squinting at the distance, and spotted the Deputy ME and Fish and Game Warden. She curled her lip at the warden, glad he couldn't see her from there and wondering if he was still mumbling about spawn and migration.

"Okay, let's send three boats left of here toward the mouth of the river, and the remaining two to the right. Split the scene and see if we can't get through this quickly. Have you seen any sign of...wildlife?" Carly wanted to tell Ben what was going on, but he would tell the chief. He was a good cop, a great teacher and leader, but god he was a stickler for the rules. He'd report it and Carly would be pulled for a psyche evaluation.

"We still looking for an overgrown pike?"

"Maybe. Something toothy like that. Or maybe a lamprey?" She tried to open his focus to include a broader range hoping if he saw anything else, he'd tell her before they found out the hard way it was tentacles.

"The boys from the sheriff's office swore they saw a huge snake earlier. Of course, Fish and Game gave them shit for about an hour, saying they wouldn't recognize a sturgeon when they saw one."

"Was it a sturgeon?" She remembered the mistaken identity from the previous day on the river.

Ben shrugged, "Probably, but I didn't see it."

He turned and walked over to the group of men to give them their orders. Carly watched as they split up. Two boats one direction, three another, and the fifth wheel walking along the ditch-line where the weeds were too thick or dry for the boats to go.

• • • • •

Donny pulled the side door closed and twisted the handle, double-checking he'd locked it. He turned and nodded to Mikey in the squad car.

"If you need anything else, Mr. Manning, I'll be happy to help you out during business hours." The reporter had been in the morgue for the last two hours getting the details *just right* so he could print the gory truth and give residents nightmares.

"*Parker*, for Pete's sake, Donny."

Donny saw the pleading look but his resolve matched his New York attitude when he was being stubborn. "You'll be Parker again when Carly says so. Until then, when she's not around asking the questions… *this?*" Donny pointed a finger back and forth between himself and Parker, "This is a professional relationship between the local news and the medical examiner's office."

"Okay, fair enough." Parker raised his hands to signal his surrender. "Thanks for the information you *did* give me though. It was very helpful."

Donny pulled the door open on Mikey's squad car and climbed into the front seat, hanging Parker's gratitude out there without a response. "Thanks for doing this, Mikey. " He pulled the door shut and they pulled out. He saw Parker shake his head in the side mirror as they drove away from him.

"Sorry for the requested quick escape, but I didn't want him following and getting in the way."

"No problem. Carly told me to help you if you needed, so I'm here." Mikey pulled onto Hammond and headed toward the Nemadji River. "So, what are we off to do?"

"I need to get inside that cavern." Donny watched the city pass by outside his window.

"Wait, *inside* the cavern?" Mikey's eyes widened. "I

am not going back in that water."

"You don't have to, just stay outside and watch for—" Donny caught himself. He'd almost said something to Mikey that would have let him know exactly what they were up against, but Carly, Parker and Donny were still keeping the crazy to themselves. "Snake, pike, sturgeon… whatever critter is messing with these bodies. Any ripples or movement in the water, I figure you can warn me."

"Okay." Mikey nodded. "As long as I don't have to go in that water."

CHAPTER THIRTY

"Is that…?" Carly felt her stomach flip and was suddenly glad she'd missed lunch.

The two sheriff deputies, in the boat closest to the river, had hollered like they'd seen a ghost. Ben and Carly had run from near the trucks. The warden and Deputy ME ran from the bridge. By the time Carly got there, the young examiner was already squatted down in the weeds looking at wounds.

"So?" Carly pressed him to speak.

"Yup, it's our FedEx driver." The young examiner answered what he thought was Carly's question, but the purple and black uniform made it obvious which driver they had found.

"But are those marks consistent with our suspected animal attacks?" Carly blinked, and chewed on her own words. She couldn't believe she had said that with a note of conviction in her voice—almost as if she believed it was nothing but an animal attacking out of sickness, confusion or hunger, as it had been suggested to those helping with the search.

He shrugged and pushed the clothing around on the body, exposing the upper arm, neck area, and reached for the pant leg. "Yes, and no. There are some strange punctures, and oh!" He jumped back as the body rolled in the water, turning over and exposing the bones showing through shredded meat.

The man's skin had a darker, more exotic, look than just that of a well-tanned Caucasian. But it didn't matter what color his skin had labeled him on his driver's license. Once it's soaked in the water, chewed on, sliced open, and left to be shredded by any other fish that come by for a quick snack, all flesh looked white. Almost gray, like the bones. However, the bones were just naturally that color, the flesh was bloodless at this point and that's what caused the horrific color. The driver's leg looked like something Carly had seen during shark week, when they put big chunks of meat on hooks and dragged them behind the boat.

The ME put both hands palms up, as if to present the evidence in front of him. "Well, he's been chewed on. That's for sure."

"Cause of death?"

"Drowning or blood loss I would guess, depending on which came first." The young ME stood up and looked around.

Carly saw the warden's eyes narrow at the body. "That ain't fish marks, Detective Manning."

"Well, maybe…" She remembered what Donny had told her to use, "But I'm just a detective. We'll send the body down to Donny and let him clean them up and get a good look at them. Then we'll know. I'm sure if it's questionable, he'll call you for references and your wildlife expertise." She smiled at him the same way she smiled at drinking men who tried to make a pass at her—be polite on the outside while knowing on the inside, *it ain't never gonna happen.*

"No signs of anything else?" She turned to each man, and watched as they shook their heads in turn. It reminded her of the wave at a football game, but horizontal rather than vertical. "It's getting dark. We're gonna call this." She saw Parker pull up on the shoulder and wave at her.

"Someone's coming for those trucks, right?" She turned and raised eyebrows at Ben.

"Tow trucks should be here any second. Taking them to impound for now."

"Well, alright then. Not much else we can do." She

put a shoulder on the ME. "Warden here can help you bag this and get it back to Donny. The rest of them can head on out. Park the boats at the marina and check in with us in the morning, just in case the chief decides he wants us to do the whole stretch one more time."

Carly smiled, knowing the warden was still stuck on the fact that she'd volunteered him for gore duty. Yes, it was an abuse of the power she had being in charge on this one, but it was worth it. *Too bad Lucas isn't out here. That would have been precious.*

She walked over to Parker's car and he rolled the window down without getting out.

"Gone fishing for Cala-Mary? Get it? Calamari but it's Mary because it's the mother?"

"Oh that's bad, Parker. Jesus, that's really bad."

"No, not Jesus. *Mary.*" He smiled wide enough at his own comment she couldn't decide if he was being silly or had been off drinking.

"The first mother was Eve." Carly offered and ruined his pun. "Cala-Eve doesn't work."

"No. No it doesn't. So, is that what this is? Looking for her? I thought they gave up when Mikey headed back to the Donny's magical lab of death and dismemberment."

"I can always tell when you're working on a piece. Your conversation gets all colorful and poetic."

Parker grinned and shrugged, Carly continued.

"But yeah, fishing. Less for her, more for her victims. Got two more." She nodded at the trucks behind him. "One driver for each. Found one, the other is still AWOL."

"Eaten?" Parker glanced at the crew starting to disperse.

"The FedEx guy had definitely been chewed on. The legs again. I gotta wonder if the meat is better or something. But no signs of the other one."

"You know, a lot of animals kill and bring the food back to their dens for later…" Parker looked up river. "Ya think…?"

"Maybe. But we dredged that cavern and all around the cemetery. Maybe she's got somewhere else she's storing them?"

"Well I'd say ask Granny Two Fingers but apparently she decided to take a walk-about. That Merwin character, and oh he's a damn joy by the way, said he hasn't seen her since yesterday but it's not unusual for her to take off like that. He said, the last time she did this she walked all the way out to the graves on the point on some sort of holy journey thing."

"To the point? That's a hike for an old lady."

"That's a hike for me and I like to think I might still be in okay shape." Parker shook his head at the idea of it. "So I'm heading home to work on this article. Dinner thoughts?"

"I'll be there in a bit. We can just order a pizza then."

Parker opened his mouth to speak and Carly could almost hear his thoughts, his intention, his words spoken of habit. But he stopped himself, closed his mouth, nodded and pulled away. Carly stood on the side of the road and realized she kind of wished he had said it.

• • • • •

The high water turned the rock and clay shoreline into a small wading path. Donny scooted awkwardly, his large frame not meant for the grace and finesse of sneaking along a ledge of any size. Mikey had planned on staying in the round parking area at the bottom of the dirt road, but he wouldn't have a clear view of the cavern from there, so he'd agreed to go with and stay outside.

"What are you going to do?" Mikey sounded openly nervous.

"Just get some samples. The wounds have been washed clean. If I can find scales or sloughed skin or anything with DNA, that would help immensely."

"Sloughed? Like a *snake*? Are these freaking monster snakes doing this? I don't do *snakes*, Donny!" Mikey started to watch the water with a concentrated intensity, pointing his gun everywhere his eyes went.

"Honestly, I don't think snakes." Donny knew he could relieve the kid's anxiety, but he also knew the truth was so much worse than any snake that would live in the north, indigenous or not.

Donny ducked under the lip, turned back at Mikey and grinned. "Be right back. Watch the—"

A black tentacle shot out from the cavern and wrapped around Donny, pulling him inside hard enough to bend him at the waste. He dropped his bag. His eyes widened and met with Mikey's. Terror on the young officer's face told Donny the kid thought it *was* a snake.

"Shoot it, Mikey. Shoot the damn thing!" Donny heard his voice echo and realized he hadn't had a chance to say that outside and only got it out of his mouth once he'd been pulled into the cavern.

Donny felt other tentacles under the water brush against his legs. He fought to break free of the single tentacle, which held him just loose enough to allow him to turn, and he was suddenly facing the creature he'd been seeing the handy work of all week.

The first thing he noticed were the eyes—silver, like liquid mercury. Perhaps the lightness of them appeared so striking because of the pure black hair framing the angular face. The cave was only dimly lit by the lowering sun, and the shadows inside seemed to swallow much of the creature's features and form. He tried to take it all in, but it was the teeth that held his attention.

When he'd told Carly, *your worst childhood nightmare monster*, he had not been joking. And now he saw that was about as apt a description as he could have given without a police sketch artist to draw it. The long thin razor blades of teeth mashed together over and over, as she moved them in a hypnotically terrifying manner. He wondered if it was the equivalent of licking its lips before a meal and decided he was *not* a meal.

"Mikey, get your scrawny ass in here and shoot this bitch!"

As if on cue, Mikey's face appeared at the overhang. His gun out in front of him.

"What the fuck is *that*?" His mouth opened, his upper lip pulling back away from his teeth in a mixed expression of disgust and disbelief. He fired once. The shot echoed in Donny's ears but the unsatisfactory *thud* he'd heard directly afterward let him know the bullet had hit the clay wall, not the creature.

The creature cocked her head at the intruder. Donny wondered if she knew Mikey was armed, but remembered Granny's claim it was immortal, that nothing could kill it, and they had to somehow trap it. He wasn't telling Mikey that, and he couldn't believe it himself. Not at the moment.

"Shoot it!"

Without losing a grip on Donny, the creature hissed and two longer tentacles shot straight out toward Mikey. Donny saw several things at once and blinked trying to process them all.

The creature had indeed knocked the gun free from the officer's hand, making Donny believe she had known it was a weapon. The gun hit the wall in what looked like slow motion, and then fell into the muddy water to sink out of sight.

The two tentacles that went for Mikey were different than the ones moving around like worms on hot pavement near Donny. The appendages by Donny were simply black tentacles, not unlike an octopus, with what appeared to be a single row of suction cups underneath and a soft tapered end. The two that went for Mikey, however, were tipped with a flat pad of hard-looking flesh, possibly a heavy cartilage or just calloused from use. Underneath the pad was a single claw that looked more like a thick talon than anything that belonged in the water. He also noted the two tentacles with the pad-claw combo came from the creature's shoulders. They were her arms.

This is not a mythological Cecaelia, Donny thought. But it was *close.* It wasn't a completely *human* upper body, only the torso and head. *All* of the limbs, including the arms, were aquatic in nature. And the exceedingly thin torso looked almost sickly, nothing like the drawings and carvings they had researched. No curves to support a bikini and sunbathe seductively on a rock. This was a sick patient lashing out at anyone near it.

Mikey pulled another gun from behind him, making Donny smile because the kid was prepared for war. He shot twice in rapid succession. One bullet hit the ceiling and the other hit one of the tentacles near Donny. Then the pad-claws on both tentacles opened and slapped Mikey on either side of the head, piercing his temples.

Donny watched as Mikey's mouth opened. He could see the scream in the young officer's eyes, but Mikey made no sound. Donny saw Mikey's eyes go thankfully blank moments before the creature forcefully pulled her claws through his cheeks and out his chin, opening his skull and face on both sides, pouring blood and brains into the muddy waters of the cavern.

Donny turned away from Mikey, powerless to help and unable to watch, and looked for another way out. Instead, Donny saw three walls made of mud and tree root, clumps of clay and what could be broken coffin boards poking through in a couple of places. Along one wall was a natural shelf. The ledge, which sat only inches above the water, was slick looking, wet with water lapping against it. Almost hidden against the wall there was a small pile of weeds and mud and what looked like a red flannel shirt. Sitting off-kilter in the middle of it was a broken egg. A small, black and pink pile of muscle and slime hung out of the hole in the side of it. He realized what he was looking at and panicked.

Killing her was definitely a priority. But her being real meant everything else Granny Two Fingers said could be real. And that meant whatever was in that egg and any others like it, had to be destroyed.

Donny frantically wiggled, trying to get out of her grip and edge closer to the ledge. There was a long stick there that looked like a cane. He knew he could use it for a weapon if he could just reach it. He flailed, slapping and punching at the tentacle that had him by the waist. He clawed and scratched at it, feeling the flesh of the creature's tentacle under his fingernails but knowing it wasn't doing enough. He bent down to bite the tentacle, thinking it his only recourse. Instead of connecting with the thick fleshy muscle of her tentacle, he found himself biting at empty air as he was suddenly out of the water.

She wrapped two more tentacles around him and held him mid-air for a moment, a foot out of the water, watching him in a way that felt to Donny like she was judging him. She slammed him suddenly against the ceiling of their cavern. He felt the loose roots from above dig into his sides hard enough for him to hear what he *hoped* was the *tree root* breaking. He heard bits of clay fall to the water like a shower of pebbles. She threw him toward the ledge, releasing him at the last moment to send him tumbling like a clumsy child into the back wall with enough force that he saw stars for a moment and grabbed his leg as pain shot through his thigh.

She turned back to the body of Mikey, lazily gliding toward his unmoving corpse as if Donny were no longer a threat. Donny tried to move and froze, the pain so intense it took his breath.

He realized she was right. He wasn't a threat to her, not in his current condition. At least one leg was broken, and quite possibly a rib or three. He looked at his side and gingerly poked through his shirt, barely holding back the scream he'd invited. He was officially broken and stuck where he was. Instead of trying to get away, he reached for his phone. The screen was cracked but still came to life when he hit the button.

He heard a hiss and looked up. The creature dropped Mikey on the ledge next to him. The young officer's body looked fine, intact, untouched. But the damage to both sides of his head was so unbelievable. *And done with nothing more than a claw?* Donny fell backward, holding his breath against the pain in his ribs and acted like he had passed out, if not died.

He needed to warn Carly. He needed to make sure he and Mikey weren't just victims. Through his lashes, he watched the creature slip back into the shadows by the entryway. As she did, her tentacles flicked all over the small cavern kicking up dirt and mud in several small swirls. To his left he saw movement and opened his eyes in horror as he watched Granny Two Fingers bob to the surface like an apple that had suddenly found its buoyancy.

He remembered the phone in his hands and hit the messaging app. He tapped the ongoing conversation with Carly, and added to the bottom in all caps. *IT'S A NEST*

Silver eyes flashed in front of him for only a moment before he saw a black tentacle coming from the side. He felt the tentacle slap his face and push him into the wall. He saw the mouth full of horrible teeth. He heard what sounded like rushing water as he blacked out.

CHAPTER THIRTY-ONE

Carly stared at the half-melted cubes in her glass. She moved the straw back and forth through them in an unintentional pattern, as her mind jumped from topic to topic with each clink of ice. *Men and monsters, that's my life.* She allowed a thin smile to barely slip across her face before it came right back in to a grimace.

"You want me to put a couple cherries in there to make it look better? Or would a lime convince you it was something else?" Jen smiled but Carly didn't look up to see it. The bartender raised one eyebrow in a high arc of almost comical reach. "That bad?"

Carly shrugged.

"I'll leave you alone." Carly heard the disappointment in Jen's voice but was lost in the storm of thoughts.

Carly wasn't in the bar to drink. Not this time. She'd run that course. Sometime between breakfast and knowing what the inside of a human thigh looked like when it was shredded underwater, she had realized it had been several days since she'd had a drop, acknowledging her four-month stint as a wannabe alcoholic was officially over. But with Parker back in the house, and him a *big* part of the thoughts currently playing Ping-Pong in her brain, she couldn't go home and think. She needed quiet. And somehow, she could find it in a crowded bar.

Her phone dinged a message and she pulled it from her pocket, expecting it to be Parker wondering about the pizza promised to him two hours ago. Instead the screen said, Donny, with a little message icon. She swiped the screen to unlock her phone and open the messaging app. IT'S A NEST was all he sent. Nothing else.

What's a nest? Where? Jesus, did he find something inside one of those bodies? Oh god, that's just gross. And I am just about done with gross.

She texted back three question marks and set it on the counter, watching the screen for a few minutes, waiting patiently for the word bubble to let her know he was typing a response. She grabbed her glass and sipped from the straw, watching the phone screen from the corner of her eye. After what felt like an eternity she snatched the phone off the counter roughly, like it was the phone's fault he hadn't replied.

"Jesus, Donny. You can't say that in all caps and then not respond." She hit the phone icon in the upper right of the message screen and lifted the phone to her ear. It rang five times and went to voice mail.

Okay, you're obviously busy and I get that.

She shook her head and dialed again.

It's a nest?

Again it went to voice mail.

"What the hell, Donny—" She stopped her intended lecture. Her jaw dropped as her eyes widened and the possibility of what he'd done and where he was dawned on her, solidifying in both probability and expectations before she finished the entire thought. *Oh shit, oh shit, oh shit, oh shit... that crazy asshole took his New York attitude to the home of the mother of all monsters!*

"I gotta jet, Jen. What's the damage?"

Jen turned, looked at Carly's face with an open mouth the detective imagined was about to say an amount, but instead opened further in a surprised circle. She shooed Carly out with her hands. Carly could only imagine the look she may have had on her face to incite that kind of response from Jen. "Go. Go! I'll tab it. Cover it later."

Between the bar stool and her car, Carly dialed Donny's number three more times. She wanted to be wrong. She wanted it to be something disgusting inside a body. She wanted it to be *anything* other than Donny at the cemetery being all exploratory and dead. She almost threw the phone in frustration, but thumbed the phone icon and tapped blindly at the top of the screen, knowing full well who the first name listed in her favorites was. Parker picked up on the first ring.

"Did you *forget* the pizza?" In better circumstances she would have heard the smile in his voice, but instead cut him off.

"Get to the cemetery. Get there now. Meet me there. But, Parker…do *not* get out of your car." Her words were jumbled and ran together in a panic that sped up her speech, as if she were an addict on uppers.

"Carly?"

"Fucking Donny. That stubborn fucking asshole went to the cavern. Him and his damn samples. And now he won't answer his phone. Just get there."

"Jesus. Okay, I'm gone. See you in a few."

Carly didn't say goodbye or thank him or even acknowledge that Parker was on board with the seriousness of this. Ben's voice in her head reminded her that Mikey had gone to *help Donny with something.*

"Oh for fuck's sake."

She scrolled with her thumb and hit the button to dial Mikey, as she turned onto East 2nd without using her blinker and pulling out in front of a slower driver who honked at her rudeness. She realized she probably should have put the magnetic emergency light on top of the car, but hadn't and didn't care if she was speeding. Any other cops who saw her and wanted to follow were welcome to do so.

Mikey's phone went to voice mail and she did throw her phone at the passenger door this time. "Fuck! Why Donny? Why the fuck would you…" She couldn't finish the sentence or the thought that went with it.

Reaching over to the passenger floor and almost sideswiping a parked car in the process, she retrieved the phone and dialed Detective Andrew Ross. Ross hated her as much as the rest of the boys club, claiming she'd ranked too fast in the field, and fought her along the way on *everything* she'd ever brought before any of them. But he lived in Allouez and could be at that cemetery in under three minutes. His phone rang once before going to voice mail and she knew he had hit DECLINE.

"Asshole."

She sped through the small stretch of businesses at the outskirts of East End and turned right onto 31st. Lights came up fast behind her and followed her into the cemetery. She drove straight back toward the small hill that led down to the river and parked the car right next to the founders' stone. She got out and spun, seeing Parker slamming his car door and lightly jogging to her side.

"What the fuck, Carly?"

"I don't... I don't fucking know. Donny sent me a text that said, *It's a nest.* That's all. And I realized he's been talking about coming down here and I've dissuaded him several times. Now he's not answering. Mikey's not answering and, according to Ben, he was supposed to be *with* Donny. And there's fucking Mikey's squad car!" She pointed behind her, indicating the car in the parking area at the bottom of the hill.

"Does Mikey even know what's going on?" Parker looked around the graveyard, fear crawling into his expression.

"No. No he doesn't. Didn't. Fuck, I don't know. Maybe Donny told him." She threw her arms up in an exaggerated pantomime of giving up.

"Okay, okay. Calm down, we'll—"

"Calm down? You're kidding, right?" She started walking down the hill as she barked her grievances. "This is *my* case and the officers helping are *my* responsibility, but it's not a normal fucking case. Do I get a serial killer who hates cops? No! I get a fucking mythical creature eating citizens. And that crazy New York fucker came down here. And he brought Mikey. And they went in that hole!" She stopped and pointed at the edge of the cavern.

The sun, while not below the horizon yet, was below the trees of the cemetery and casting long shadows across the river and the opening to the cavern, which suddenly looked very much like a mouth to Carly.

"Fuck!" She put her hands on either side of her mouth to cup the sound, "Donny! Mikey!"

She pulled her .40 caliber Smith and Wesson MP9 from her side, pulled the slide to load the chamber, and glanced back at Parker. "Did you bring a weapon?"

"I have a knife…" He reached for his back pocket.

"You always have a knife…"

CHAPTER THIRTY-TWO

"Do you see anything?" Carly skimmed the water with her flashlight. She knew she'd never see the cecaelia in the murky water with the sun so low, but perhaps she'd see the ripples, the motion in the water itself.

"No. Looks clear out here."

"I'm going in."

"Jesus, Carly. You sure we shouldn't call—"

She heard him leave the thought hanging in the air and punctuate it with a sigh. *Yeah, call who?* She thought and didn't bother looking at him with the question written on her face.

His light shone past her as he ducked under the lip to join her, scanning the area as he did so. Carly heard him gasp when his light stopped on the remains of Granny Two Fingers, recognizable only by her long black braid and the single green eye staring at them.

Her face had been peeled like an orange, in neat strips, the edges of flesh that remained showed signs of sharp teeth dragging across before tearing meat from bone. The exposed skull glistened in the water, her head appearing to bob without the benefit of her small body to weigh it down.

"Granny?" Parker questioned.

"Yeah. Not missing after all. Dead."

"The Indians are *not* going to be—"

"Donny!" Carly saw the large man crumpled in a heap on what look like a ledge directly across from them. She pushed through the water in a forced power walk, not caring how much noise she made or splashing she did.

Parker kept pace with her on the left but suddenly froze. "Carly, stop!"

She froze in a position reminiscent of kids playing

Red Light Green Light—her arm outstretched in front of her as she'd been reaching for the edge of the natural shelf made of clay and tree roots. "What?" She half whispered, half hissed in irritation.

"I kicked something." His eyes were wide as he looked down at the dark water.

Oh crap, Carly looked around her, shining the light into the water and frowning as it became nothing but a blurred beam of brown mud because their walking had stirred the bottom. *Where,* she mouthed at him.

Parker pointed straight down in front of him, and Carly shook her head.

"I'm right next to you." She whispered. "If she's octopus size, I would have run into her as well."

Parker grabbed Carly's shoulder, and she watched as he slowly swept his leg back and forth, apparently feeling the bottom for safe passage. She felt him jump against her, his expression pinched and shoulders hunched up. Movement in the water in front of him caused Carly to hold her breath. Bubbles broke the surface and she pointed her gun at them, prepared to blow the cecaelia's head off when it rose.

Officer Mikey Gunderson popped out of the water like a stiff board, giving them only a moment to recognize him and absorb what was going on, before he rolled away from them and began to sink again.

Carly blinked, momentarily unwilling to accept the truth that came with the visual. Both sides of Mikey's head were horrifically torn from temple to jaw line, a gaping crater in flesh and bone, which was dark enough to appear empty.

"No! No, no, no…" Carly reached for him with her free hand and grabbed a handful of his uniform shirt, barely keeping him afloat. Parker put his hands under

Mikey's armpits and lifted him instinctively toward him, a motion he would use trying to save someone from drowning, though this body was well past dead.

Carly felt the hot tears in her eyes, as her jaw clenched. She let go of the officer's body when Parker pulled against her.

Parker took several steps toward the ledge, pulling Mikey's body with him.

Carly held her handgun out with both hands and turned in a circle, watching the water for any activity. She glanced at Granny Two Fingers' head still floating casually near the entrance and took it as a sign the water hadn't been disturbed enough to send her adrift through the opening. She turned back as Parker was pushing Mikey's body up on the ledge.

"Carly…"

Donny's voice startled her and she turned, gun still out in front of her to stare at the medical examiner who had one bloodshot eye open and focused on her.

"Jesus, Donny. You're alive?" Parker sidestepped over to him as Carly approached the ledge.

"How? Mikey and Granny and—" She didn't want to say it out loud.

Donny shook his head. "I think she thought I was dead. I thought I was too for a bit I guess." His voice was harsh, panicked, but low as he looked around. "Did you get her?"

"We haven't seen her."

"Get out of here, Carly." The fear in his eyes was something Carly had never seen or imagined was even possible.

Parker reached for him but spoke to Carly. "We'll get him out of here and send swimmers in for Mikey and Granny's bodies."

Donny yelped and pulled away from Parker. "I can't walk or even swim out of here, and we need to *not* be in here. So go get a backboard and float my ass out of here before she gets back!" Still only using one eye, the other swelled with the entire left side of his face, he suddenly appeared more alert.

"What's broke?" Carly looked him over and nodded at his leg. "Just that?"

"Leg, couple ribs, and I'm really fucking hoping not my back. Hurts like hell to try and move anything, so I don't know if it's that I *can't* move or that my body is preventing it through swelling to protect itself."

Carly nodded, "I'll call for the truck." She walked toward the entrance of the cavern to get a better signal and dialed dispatch. As she told Lucas to send an ambulance down the hill to the river at the cemetery, she listened to Donny talking to Parker.

"It really was a mythical fucking creature, Parker. But it wasn't what we looked up."

"It's not a cecaelia? Shit. What the hell is it?" Parker hopped up on the ledge and pulled his feet out of the water, situating himself between Donny and Mikey's body to block the view of the corpse Donny's eye seemed locked on.

"It's close I guess. From the neck up you would think it was a woman, though the cheekbones are super angular and the eyes are silver and creepy as hell. From the neck to hip, it's human-*ish,* I guess, but it's thin. *Really* thin. Like wannabe runway model anorexia thin."

"Well, it hasn't eaten for five hundred years."

"Point taken. But its ribs stick out. You could actually count them. And the collarbone is almost pointy. This was no voluptuous mermaid cousin. Below that? Yup, tentacles. Fuck me, there were goddamn tentacles. Black.

Looked like snakes almost. Except the top two—the two that are her arms—those things are *fucking* horrible. They're longer and at the end…" Donny's gaze drifted away for a moment. "They're like mittens almost. Flat on the one side, and then the thumb is actually a claw or talon or something like that. A nasty, black, hooked claw. That's what she used on Mikey. Went right through his head with a slap." Donny looked at Carly as she returned to the ledge. "That was the absolute worst noise I've *ever* heard. And I'm from New York, where they pretty much invented horrible noises."

"Help's coming, Donny. We just gotta keep everyone in one piece for a few." Carly reached up and patted his shoulder gently.

"You see that shit behind me?"

Carly shook her head and leaned, looking past him.

"Oh fuck." Parker said what Carly hadn't had time to put into words.

"A nest." Carly nodded and looked at Donny. "That the only one?"

"That I've seen."

"Fuck. Okay. Between that possibility, a dead officer, a broken ME… I *gotta* go see the chief and tell him the truth."

"You want help?" Parker offered.

Carly turned her back to the boys and watched the water. "I don't know that anyone or anything can help me say what I actually have to say out loud."

CHAPTER THIRTY-THREE

The chief of police, head in his hands, splayed his fingers and looked at Carly through them. "Are you *fucking* kidding me?"

Carly just shook her head. She had no more words. She'd explained how the high water had eroded the bank and exposed the coffins and mass grave, and with those things, set the creature free. She'd shown him pictures of the fresh kills and the wounds they presented, and how Donny had matched them to cephalopods. She'd told him everything Granny Two Fingers had told her about the myth. And once they'd stabilized Donny, he told the chief what he'd seen.

The chief had been speechless on the bench outside Donny's hospital room for almost twenty minutes when he finally spoke to question the reality of it all.

"I should fire you, you know that?" He pulled his hands away and turned to face her.

"Why? How could we have done any better if you'd have known?"

"Well I sure as hell wouldn't have let Donny—"

"You couldn't have stopped Mr. New York anymore than I could. Plus, he's Chief Medical Examiner. He's not your employee to boss around. He's elected."

"Fuck. Fuck, Carly. This is a fucking mess."

"I know…" She looked up as Parker exited Donny's room. "How is he?"

"Drugged." Parker looked between the chief and Carly, "Should I maybe leave you two alone?"

"No, Mr. Manning. Matter of fact, have a seat. You were part of all this, this bullshit and secrecy. Maybe you can offer some way to fucking fix it."

"Well," Carly could tell Parker was trying to appear

calm. "I guess I would say go to her, and bring all the big guns. Donny said Mikey got a couple shots off before she disarmed him. The one that hit her did damage. And she knew it was a weapon, which means she's afraid of it."

"She? We're referring to this thing as a *she*?" The chief rolled his eyes.

"It is a female, Chief. Kind of *the* female in a sense."

"Yeah well, I'm divorced twice for a reason. Some females are bitches. And this bitch needs to die."

Carly blinked at him and chewed at her upper lip, thinking. She'd never seen the chief this pissed before. And she'd never heard him talk about any ex-wives or even women in general with such hatred before.

"Should we call in the guard, maybe?" Carly offered, trying to force the chief to get past the shock of it all and engage in a plan.

He shook his head, "Nah, we can handle this. You said it had tentacles and human eyes?"

"No, Donny said that. But I believe him. Fuck, Chief, I don't know. I mean if we call in all the city boys, the county crew, and Fish and Game... I mean, even if it is a legend, it's still just an animal."

"And it can die?"

"God I hope so."

"And which God is that? The One in the *good book*, or one of these crazy monster gods that come lay eggs with this thing?"

"It'll work." She ignored the chief's overreaction to the idea of legends and myths. "Donny said she was wounded. Some wicked looking puncture in her chest and a slash on her side, besides what Mikey did. We have a lot of men with weapons—"

"Throw in some angry Indians as soon as they find out about Granny Two Fingers. I'm sure they'll want to help." Parker held his hand out palm up like he was offering something.

"True. So that's what? Three dozen men and women? We pull out the riot gear and arm ourselves to the teeth." Carly shrugged like it made perfect sense.

"How the fuck do we tell the boys what they're fighting?"

"Well, that's why they pay *you* the big bucks." Carly patted his shoulder. "I would suggest putting them in a conference room. All of them. Place mandated gag orders on the lot of them. Then show them the photos Donny has of the wounds, of what this thing can do. I'm pretty sure no matter what we call it, they don't want to be dead, so they'll pay attention."

"I guess. I mean, what else are we going to do." The chief looked at Parker and squinted one eye before he returned his gaze to Carly. "And nothing goes across the radios. Fucking reporters with scanners will come crawling out of the swamp and get eaten."

Parker put his arms up in a motion of surrender, "I promise not to tell a soul."

Carly glared at him, *yeah because you want the scoop.*

"I won't even write about it until we sit down after and decide what we even want to tell the public. If anything."

Carly was impressed. Parker was being human rather than a reporter, and she saw the chief's expression as he recognized it as well.

"So when? What's the feeding schedule of this thing? The boys out fishing were mid-morning, but the mustang couple was evening. How do we know when that thing is even in the cavern?"

"Daytime would be best to see, because I *hate* that in the movies. They never wait until daylight. But damn it, she's probably out and about during the day hunting and such, and it'll be easier to trap her inside there at night."

"Christ. Nighttime. You know how dark it gets on that river? There are no street lights over by the cemetery at all."

Carly nodded, thinking.

"What about light towers and construction lamps and such? Couldn't you light it up? I mean, wait until dark." Parker leaned forward, talking with his hands like there was a map of the area in front of him. "Maybe have someone sit and watch with binoculars for movement in the water so we know when she's in there. Then drop weighted nets in a couple different places up stream *and* down stream, so she can't go shooting out into the river. Then hit the power and light the whole area up..."

"And shoot the living shit out of her." Carly finished his thought.

The chief nodded, "Might work. I should probably talk to Scott over at Fish and Game. He may have some ideas."

Carly snarled, she really couldn't stand that little louse of a man. "Yeah? You think he has a lot of experience with what? Octopus? Or mythical squid-women?"

"He doesn't have experience with *human* women." Parker added and winked at Carly.

"Well, he and his boys will be involved. But yeah, you're right. And he's kind of a horrible warden. I could see him spilling the whole thing. I better have someone find me an inter-department gag order for the mayor to sign. Going against that will cost him his job, his rep, everything. Should keep him quiet."

"Okay then. So tonight?" Carly was eager to be done with it all.

"Can we tell if she's in there yet or not?" The chief

stared at her a moment and she wondered if he was ever going to blink.

She shook her head, feeling suddenly defeated. "No."

"No." The chief agreed. "So this is what we'll do. I'm going to tell Sparks exactly what happened to Mikey. He'll be all about revenge but you know Ben, he'll be calm as hell about it. I'll put him and a rookie on watch duty overnight tonight. We'll see if we can't keep her— Christ, now I'm calling it a her! We'll see if we can't keep *it* from attacking anyone else tonight. In the morning, we'll get everyone together. Set ground rules. Load for bear, or in this case, really thick octopus. Get out there and set up with nets ready to drop—what, three places on either side?"

Carly nodded, "Set up the lights everywhere during the day while she's out and about."

"And wait for the sun to go down and for mommy to come slithering home." The chief smiled and Carly relaxed, he was on board and felt good about the plan he was calling his. Perfect. "In the morning, *you* need to go out and get us some additional bodies with weapons from Allouez. You think the tribe will listen? Help?"

"Once I tell them it took Granny Two Fingers, I think they'll be more than eager." Carly stood. "I'm going to sit with Donny for a bit.

"Okay then, I'll see you in the morning. Deal with Allouez and bring them with you. We'll meet, all bodies involved, in the fourth floor conference room of the court house at ten sharp."

"Got it." She watched the chief stand and shuffle down the hall, his shoes making a soft whisper as they went.

"You know, Carly, I saw this movie…" Parker looked

into her eyes and she could feel him trying to burrow past them into her head.

"Don't talk like that, Parker. Don't jinx it with bad thoughts and make that your reality." She'd used his own line about reality on him without even thinking about it.

He stared at her for another moment. "Okay. Positive thoughts. This will work." He nodded at Donny's door, "You want me to wait for you or just meet you at home?"

"If you wouldn't mind, I'd appreciate it if you waited." She turned and opened the door.

Donny's voice called into the hallway, "Parker, you still out there?"

Parker poked his head inside, "Not Mr. Manning? Carly give me clearance again?"

"Nah, you saved my skin. I gave you clearance. Just wanted to say thanks. Couldn't remember if I did or not."

She pulled the door shut and smiled. *Yep, they've got him drugged up. That's the fourth time he's thanked Parker.*

CHAPTER THIRTY-FOUR

Carly had no fingernail left on her index finger. She'd been chewing on it for the better part of the last hour. Waiting. Patiently. For nothing to happen.

The day had gone smoother than she expected thus far, and she found herself *knocking on wood* every time she thought that. The tribe had been visibly upset with the news, yet surprisingly calm, as if they'd been waiting for Granny to go down against *something*. The meeting with all departments went well, considering the chief had to stop a handful of times for whispering and nay saying questions. In the end, it was Donny's photos and testimony that removed all doubt. Not a single officer in the county didn't trust Donny Meys. His word was good and his reputation was strong. As one officer put it, "If Donny says there's a monster, then there's a *fucking* monster."

The men split up after the meeting, some to get to work, others to rest for the overnight. The chief had spent the early morning hours going over the range records for every officer and sheriff in the town. He split the crew into two: a team to set up and another to destroy.

Those with less skill on the range, or whom the chief didn't want on the water at night for whatever reasons he had deemed logical—from weak swimmers to family men and women—were in charge of setting everything up, getting all the boats and lights ready, as well as maintaining patrol routes and a sense of normalcy in town.

Conversely, those with special skills, worthy talents, or—as Carly noticed when she saw some of the names— less to lose, would be on the night shift to take the creature down. The crews had finished set up shortly before six o'clock. It was now eight and the sunset was an almost ironic vibrant red.

For the eighth time since she'd positioned herself on the side of the small hill that led to the parking area by the river and offered her the best view of the cave, she ticked off the men and where they were.

Seven of the Allouez tribe members showed up to the meeting with a rifle and a pistol each. Each one was a registered gun owner and had a permit for conceal carry. This immediately alleviated any worries the chief may have had, as that meant they'd all had background checks and records on file. He put four of them at the mouth of the Nemadji, two on either side, to watch for Gete-Oga to come in, and to be the final layer of protection should she try to get out that way. The other three were on either side of the bridge, with one lookout on the bridge itself, and were the warning system to let the cops know if she was coming in, or their tribe members if she was escaping.

Between the bridge and the cavern were three sets of officers spaced about two hundred yards apart. The first two were Fish and Game, the next two were County Sheriffs, and the final two were Superior Police Department. These teams were set and ready with weighted nets, to be dropped the moment she passed the next duo, so she wouldn't realize it until she was well beyond the splash it would make. There were three sets of men on the other side of the graveyard, heading upstream, in case she came in from that way. Whichever way she did *not* come, all three nets would be dropped the second she was spotted at the other end. These were meant to trap her in the middle and safeguard against her getting out of the river. Each net would be illuminated with a spotlight *only* if she headed back toward them, so she could be seen and taken out. Otherwise they would remain dark, and hopefully unnoticed and unnecessary.

Two SWAT members were above what was now being referred to as *the lair*. The prep team had run charges down into the cavern. Two into the water just inside and two tangled into the root above the water line. They were not meant to kill the creature, but rather disorient her with percussion charges in the water, and flash charges above. The underwater charges were a very mild depth charge, almost a big firecracker, because there was too much concern over whether or not a full depth charge would drop the side of the riverbed and another round of coffins into the river. Each of the two SWAT members held the detonators for one of each type of charge, and hoped to hit them at the same time when she went inside, perfectly executing a double strike against her. If they could momentarily blind or deafen her, then the team would have an advantage. It had been a great addition to the plan, and left in the hands of the SWAT team as northern Wisconsin seemed to be almost devoid of bomb squads, the closest being almost five hours and six counties away, and the chief neither wanted to wait nor tell them why they should come.

Across from the lair, in full view of the SWAT team on high ground, were five boats—three rescue boats and two fishing boats owned by officers. Each boat had been pushed carefully into the weeds on the other side of the river, out of the open water and almost dry docked in the thick marsh. This was to both keep away from the creature, and have the best view for attack. Each boat had a generator and construction floodlight, as well as three heavily armed officers.

The spotters would drop nets. The SWAT would disorient her. And then the brigade would flip the lights on, blinding her but providing ample light for the teams, and attempt to take her out with precision strikes. The strongest shooters in town were in those five boats. Those men were the core of the mission.

The chief was near the top of the small hill, shouting distance from the SWAT teams, and able to see all five boats. All officers had open mikes on and the chief had a bullhorn for emergencies. Carly was on the side of the hill across the gravel road from the chief and SWAT, watching the entrance as an additional spotter, and also to warn or relay from the upriver team. Parker was positioned halfway up the hill with night vision binoculars at the ready and still no weapon. He was only there because he'd begged. He was told not to engage in anything but to stand lookout and relay anything he saw. On the high ground on the other side of the lair, out of Carly's range of view, was the warden, looking out on that side much like Carly was on this.

They were set up. They were ready. Hell, if the guys were feeling anything at all like Carly was, they were twitching to shoot the hell out of this bitch if she would just show her face.

And then the mike squawked.

Carly stood and looked intently down river as she heard one of the officers finger his mike and whisper in a panic.

"Net two, net two. Just saw black mass pass by. Waiting for net three to call it to drop net. Net three, copy?"

"Net three, we're watching."

"Nets four, five and six, drop now." The chief's voice threw the command to the upriver teams.

There was silence and Carly held her breath, waiting for the team on the third net to spot it, so net two could trap it. The anticipation in the air was almost palpable. The fear in her mouth tasted a lot like copper and she realized she was chewing on her lip a little too hard.

"Drop drop drop. This is net three, it passed us. No, wait. Shit. Don't drop. Repeat, don't drop!"

Carly leaned out and stared down river.

"Chief, that was a fucking *sturgeon*. Goddamned sheriff called it on a sturgeon." The officer on the mike sounded familiar but Carly couldn't place him. She looked up the hill at the chief and saw his face go red, matching the sun setting behind him.

"Christ, okay." The irritation in the chief's voice was unmistakable. "Everyone pull your nets up and reset. Be quick about it, and be careful guys. We may only get one shot at this before she decides to hit open water and be gone. Don't fuck it up again."

As he spoke, Carly turned back to the river in time to see the splash. She watched as three tentacles gracefully arced through the air before slipping into the water, as the creature dove down and entered the cavern.

"Chief!" Carly whispered into her mike and pointed.

"I got it, Greene." The officer directly across from her in the fourth boat held up a thumb to her, and she watched the other two officers in his boat pull their rifles and set their sights on the entrance of the lair.

"Drop all nets." Chief sounded like his voice had gone up an octave. "Repeat, drop *all* nets. SWAT? Ready with charges. Boat four. Who's your spotter?"

"SWAT one ready."

"Roberts, sir. I'm watching it."

"SWAT two ready."

"You let us know if you see her come out. SWAT, blow the water charges on my count. Three. Two. One. Blow them."

The spray of water out of the mouth of the cavern came a split second before Carly heard the small explosions.

Within the sound she knew to be the percussion charges muted by water, was something else. Something like an underwater scream. And she was certain she knew what that was as well.

CHAPTER THIRTY-FIVE

Tentacles flailed on the water and the creature snapped her head back and forth as she broke the surface outside the cavern, in what appeared to be a motion meant to clear her ears. Carly's view was exhilarating and terrifying, as she could see both the pain and anger in the creature's expression as it looked around.

"Carly, get down!" The officer in the boat across the way barked the order no louder than a harsh whisper in church through the mike pinned to her shoulder. She squatted back into the brush.

"SWAT, hold flash charges. She's outside." The chief looked through night binoculars and watched. "All boats, she's in the channel. Light her up and fire at will."

The collective noise of all five generators kicking in and the large beam lights powering up made a noise like a deer snorting, a puff of angry air.

And there she was, trapped in the glow of five 6000-watt light towers.

Carly's eyes widened as she was allowed to take in all of two seconds of Gete-Oga before the creature went underwater. Donny's description had been spot on. A somewhat attractive face on the anorexic chest of a drug addled model. The sharp angle of her cheekbones glistened in the bright lights and Carly hadn't gotten a chance to see much else before she'd gone under.

Carly follow the sudden screams and watched as the light in boat three toppled into the river, the boat itself flipped and the officers were suddenly in waist deep swamp water. Their eyes were wide enough for Carly to see clearly from the opposite shore. Two officers jumped unexpectedly as their third yelped and disappeared in the weeds in a jerking motion that could only mean he was pulled away. A tentacle coming up a moment later with the officer wrapped inside it and lazily let go with a flicking motion, sending the officer flying toward the fourth boat. He took the cop closest to the end of the boat out, landing directly on him, and both of them folded over into the water in a heap.

"Shoot the fucking thing!" The chief was now screaming in the open mike.

Shots from her left pulled Carly's attention and she realized the two SWAT officers had come to the front edge of the upper bank and were on their bellies with eyes to scopes, shooting at the center of the river. She could see the bullets hitting the river but there seemed to be more fired than she could see, so she had to assume they were hitting the creature. Carly could ear the gunfire both in the air and in her open mike, which made it sound all the more impressive and as if there were twice as many people shooting.

"Ignore the tentacles, go for center mass." One of the SWAT officers gave the tip to whoever could get a shot off.

More shots came from her right and Carly turned to see boats four and five had crept out to a half-circle and were shooting at the creature currently in front of the fourth boat. Carly looked back to the water where the third boat had been and couldn't see the two officers who had still been standing in the weeds without a boat. She was about to panic when she saw feet in the air and realized they had scrambled to the second boat and were pulling themselves into it.

The gunfire suddenly stopped and she looked back to the center of the river.

No Gete-Oga. *Was she down? Did they finish her?* As if to answer her thoughts, the mike squawked to life again.

"Where'd she go?"

"I don't know. I lost her."

"Fuck! Net three, this is net three, she's coming straight at us."

"I see her!" Shots resumed, further down the river out of Carly's line of sight and she could only presume it was the first boat or the third net. What sounded like the finale at a world-class fireworks show was happening around the bend from Carly and she leaned out as far as could to see.

"Jesus, is it even hurting it?" One of the officers sounded worried. "Do we have any bazookas?" He sounded serious, but Carly knew it was frustration talking, because shooting off something like that in this kind of chaos would just ensure downed officers.

"She's gone under again."

The gunfire stopped.

"Holy shit! This is net three. She slammed us and the net held, she's heading back upstream. Net four get ready."

"Boats four and five, watch and take her out." The chief was squatting next to the SWAT officers. Off mike she heard him say to them, "Take it out at any cost." And she looked up the hill at him, not sure what he could possibly mean other than he was pre-approving sloppy targeting.

Boat four and five suddenly started shooting without saying anything and Carly saw the mass of tentacles in the river. The lights made the muddy water appear more orange than the brown of daylight. As such, the stark black of the creature's tentacles seemed to look like shadows against it. It wasn't as well lit as they would have liked, but it was enough to see what was going on.

As the gunfire continued and the tentacles flailed,

either being shot or moving to avoid the shots, Carly watched in horror as the two longer tentacle arms came out of the mass and grabbed one of the officers on the fourth boat. Just as Donny had described, it slapped the side of the man's face and pulled him into the water.

As Gete-Oga pulled him under, muffling his screams, Carly realized the creature was also screaming. The sound was somewhere between a cry and a hiss, and seemed nonstop, like a train whistle someone wouldn't let go of. The claw-tipped tentacle shot out and struck another officer, those around him on the boat frantically shooting at the mass in the water, but also at the tentacle itself. Carly watched in horror as the officers came dangerously close to cross-firing at each other, but smiled as she saw the claw-tipped tentacle fall into the water, the orange river suddenly seeming much darker.

The creature dove suddenly and the silence of paused gunfire seemed incredibly loud to Carly. She walked to the edge of river, squatted down low and looked across the water, like she used to do on the beach to locate the shine of agates in the fading sunlight. But this time, it wasn't a rock she hoping to see but a ripple in the water—an indication of where the creature had gone.

A sudden muffled splash to her left and she realized Gete-Oga had gone back in the cavern.

"She's inside!" Carly didn't use the mike, but rather just yelled to everyone within earshot but waved her arms at the boats across the way before pointing frantically. One of the SWAT officers scrambled down the hill and put a finger to his lips. From her shoulder mike she heard the other SWAT officer whisper, "shut your eyes."

Rather than shut them as told, she looked down and peripherally saw the flash grenades go off inside the cavern. No squeals or screams from inside led Carly to believe the creature had been under water at the time and the flash grenade hadn't affected her.

As the SWAT officer who had come down scooted along the edge to spy inside, he was startled and sent down on his backside. Gete-Oga came shooting out of the cavern at him. Dodging to the side, he disappeared in the darkness of the branches there. Carly screamed while wondering if the creature had night vision and could see him or not. It turned toward her and smiled, and Carly realized it could see her.

She turned to scramble up the hill as she heard Parker yelling her name from above her, running down to meet her. He pushed her into the bushes at the side, out of the way and cracked a flare. Waving it in the creature's face hoping to blind her.

Carly heard the gunfire, but the flare had a blinding affect on her and she couldn't see who was shooting and where they were aiming. Movement to the right of her showed another tentacle floating in the water, separated from the creature by several bullets.

Parker yelped and went down in front of her, dropping the flare into the water.

Carly saw the creatures remaining claw-tipped arm firmly grasping Parker's leg. She pulled up her pistol and took aim several feet away from his leg. Emptying the clip into the tentacle, Carly hadn't realized she'd blown it clean off the creature until Parker reached up and grabbed her.

"Carly, Run!" Parker rolled to the side, away from the water, holding his leg in the air. The SWAT officer who had been by the mouth of the cavern was suddenly behind the creature, his assault rifle pointed at it, firing with prejudice. Additional shots came from across the river and Carly scrambled backward, away from the target area.

Carly watched the creature as bullets shredded her, afraid to take her eyes off it. Four of the six tentacles were shot away from its body. Both upper arm tentacles dismembered. Carly wasn't sure the anatomy of the chest cavity, where the heart was, or *how many* hearts there may be. But there was enough lead in the creature to create what the boys would call *a serious leaking problem*.

No matter how tough it was, if it bled it could bleed out, and Carly watched as the expression on the creature's face came to the same conclusion.

Gete-Oga looked up to the moon, and then directly at Carly. It pulled itself closer to her, out of the water and onto the edge of the riverbank. Once it was exposed on the clay, her full length of torso plus tentacles reaching back almost twelve feet, all shooters with clear shots opened fire. The creature's body pulsed with each hit, jerking as if it were being shocked over and over again. Carly saw there were only five tentacles on the lower half, and the stub of one lost long-ago. Of the five, there remained only one attached to her hip area, where the flesh changed in a strange mottled ombre from peach to black, from light to dark, with deep red blood covering all of it.

Carly watched, as the eyes studying her blinked slowly, as if they were not going to reopen. The mouth opened slightly and Carly saw the razor sharp wicked teeth that had done so much damage. As it fell forward, no arms left to stop it from landing with a thud in the mud and clay, it smiled at Carly and made several clicking sounds. Not screams like it had before, but something else. Something that sounded more like communication than anger, and Carly wondered if the creature was *glad* to end her eternity under the hail of modern weaponry.

The silver eyes held Carly in their gaze, the body

jerking from the shots *still* being fired into it. It blinked again, slowly. It's chest rose and fell with labored breath. Carly pointed her gun at the monster at her feet, but felt all her fear and loathing for the creature slip into pity and something akin to grief. The silver eyes suddenly seemed wrong, and Carly realized they were less silver and more just white, like twin moons staring at her.

"Stop!" She cried but couldn't be heard over the gunfire. She thumbed her mike, "Stop! It's dead."

The gunfire came to a slow halt, like a popcorn bag that was almost finished, a couple here or there for good measure and then it was done. Silence filled the air, which smelled of gunpowder and adrenaline.

CHAPTER THIRTY-SIX

Carly sat on the large rock at the water's edge, watching the river lap at the blood on shore like a hungry living thing. The creature, Gete-Oga, lay mangled on the shore.

Parker appeared in front of her and offered a hand to help her up.

"Thanks. How's the leg?"

He held it out for her to see the medics had cut off the bottom of his jeans. "Only four staples, I'll live."

Carly nodded, not really hearing him as she watched the scene. Officers who had gone down had been gathered, bagged, and were being loaded into ambulances for transport to the morgue. Those remaining were mulling about like teenagers at their first dance, looking very uncertain how to process any of this. Several were poking at the tentacles lying still in the shallow waters. A couple actually took pieces, like strange flesh souvenirs. And she cocked her head as she saw one of the SWAT officers come out from the cave with the broken egg in his hands.

He saw her watching him, "Not for me. For science. Donny said grab it if we could." Carly nodded, that sounded like Donny.

The amount of gunfire had been on par with a mob massacre. And the victim lay, in bits and pieces, in a heaped pile no more than four feet away from Carly waiting to be bagged and tagged itself. Carly wasn't sure she wanted to see it under the harsh lights of a lab. She wasn't sure it shouldn't be somehow respected and pushed back into the water to decompose and become part of the eco-system it ruled.

She felt Parker thread his fingers into hers and squeeze, and she blinked back into the now. "Sorry, you said you'll be okay?"

"Yeah."

"I think maybe I should call those boys from Mackinaw. A little government cover-up right now might save all our jobs…"

"No worries. Everything will work out. And I think *we* will make it through this."

Carly looked up at him like he'd said something insane and then back at the heap of cephalopod, "Oh I'm pretty sure *she* ain't coming back from that but just her existence—"

"I didn't mean her. I didn't mean *this*." He gestured back and forth between them and stared at her for a moment, his eyes softened, dragging her with him into a completely different silent conversation.

"Oh. *That*." She squeezed his hand and sighed. "We've got some work ahead of us, but yeah, I think we'll be fine after I figure out how to let go of *that* monster." She smiled. "Meanwhile, do you *think* you can keep this *out* of the paper?"

"I could be persuaded." Parker tugged her hand gently before letting it go, suggesting she follow him up the hill. "The question is, do you think Superior will ever learn how to keep her dead?"

Carly took one last look at the monster, appearing so weak and unimportant in its defeat, and turned to follow him up the hill. "God, I hope so."

• O • O • O • O • O •

AUTHOR NOTE
aka How a writer twists things around to call it fiction

I do indeed have Ojibwa Chippewa blood from the Bad River Tribe from my Nana. And they do indeed have some great myths and legends. I invite you to check out Mishebeshu, Nibiinabe, and many others. But you will not find Gete-Oga among them. I made her up completely and slipped her right inside the mythos, because that's what writers do, with absolutely zero offense intended toward the tribe.

I did *not* however, make up the unfortunate mass grave that was created in 1918 when they moved Native bodies from Wisconsin Point to the St. Francis Cemetery on the Nemadji River. Nor did I make up the fact that the river has washed away the bank and exposed them, or that Lake Superior tends to cough up her dead. Only details were researched. I went into this knowing the rest. You see, I grew up on that beautiful lake known for its incredible temper, and as a writer, I simply embellish on the horrors she has wrought and left in my memories…

ABOUT THE AUTHOR

Born and raised in Wisconsin, Kelli Owen now lives in Pennsylvania. She's attended countless writing conventions, participated on dozens of panels, and spoken at the CIA Headquarters in Langley, VA. Visit her website at kelliowen. com for more information. F/F

Made in the USA
Monee, IL
18 February 2022